I0742894

NOIR

II

Cult

The Red Emperor

The Redhead Rip-Off

The Incident Report

JERRY BADER

Copyright © 2018 Jerry Bader

All rights reserved.

ISBN Paperback: 978-1-988647-43-2

Hard Cover: 978-1-988647-44-9, Ebook: 978-1-988647-45-6

CULT

Rita Daveed, an ex Israeli intelligence officer, becomes the business manager and partner of a Hindu mystic, Baba Bhang, who promotes his somewhat corrupted interpretation of the ancient philosophy of Charvaka: a pursuit of pleasure based on the notion that there are no Gods or afterlife.

When Rita and Baba open their American ashram in California wine country, they find themselves in a real estate conflict with the local winery owners and their industrial backers. The locals say they want to control the area's real estate market to maintain the county's wine country image when in fact their real agenda is something completely different.

THE RED EMPEROR

In the mould of the Maltese Falcon, The Red Emperor weaves a convoluted tale for the search of who killed Peter Pretty Boy Chen over a seemingly worthless Chinese gift shop souvenir, and why a group of misfit grifters are so interested.

Grist and Dime are at it again, but this time it involves the Chinese triads; a tailor that moonlights as a hit man; an ex French DGSE agent that happens to be Detective Dime's boyfriend; and a kooky group of characters right out of central casting. The question is, who killed Peter Pretty Boy Chen and why, when the prize is only a cheap statute that anyone could pick up at any Chinese souvenir shop?

THE REDHEAD RIP-OFF

Mix a gorgeous redhead with a historic name, an old man who happens to be one of the best forgers of Austrian artist Gustav Klimt, and the second son of a triad Dragon Head, and you've got a recipe for big money mayhem.

What could possibly go wrong when an oddball group of grifters attempts to con a Chinese gangster who happens to employ a group of professional confidence artists?

THE INCIDENT REPORT

USAF Major Willard White has a fatal flaw that gets him killed: he tells the truth about an unexplained encounter with an apparent alien presence. Can a disgraced reporter and his beautiful rookie partner get the story out, or will it be buried in Special Report 13?

USAF war hero, test pilot Major Willard White knew better than to file an Incident Report about an unexplained encounter while on a test flight, but what he didn't realize was the report was going to get him killed. After being threaten by his superiors and a shadowy NSA character, White attempts to protect himself by sending the report to a disgraced reporter and his beautiful rookie partner, both looking for a career-making story. Getting the story out turns out to be an exercise in maneuvering through a maze of intimidation and dead bodies resulting in an unconventional solution.

CULT

Baba's Big Bhang

JERRY BADER

MRPwebmedia.com/books

PROLOGUE

Five Years Earlier

Rita Daveed sits quietly sipping a cappuccino in The Fumoir bar, located in London's five star Claridge's Hotel. She is waiting patiently for her dinner partner Prince Fahed, Assistant Deputy of Finance in the Saudi Council of Ministers. Fahed is an important player in Middle East financial wheeling and dealing; an occupation that requires a certain amount of discretion; unfortunately, the Prince has an Achilles' heel, beautiful women. The current object of his fantasies is the exceedingly exotic Rita Daveed. Beauty may be only skin-deep, but when it attains the heights of the lovely Rita, it becomes something almost transcendental.

There are women who are attractive and women who are beautiful, and then there is Rita Daveed, an exquisite specimen of sublime perfection, a goddess, irresistible to men and most women. She is a mysterious mix of Eastern European, Sabra, and Indian heritages. She is also a Shin Bet agent for the Israeli Security Agency in the Arab Affairs Department who is currently on loan to the Mossad. Beautiful women attract attention, the perfect asset when trying to corrupt the Assistant Deputy of Finance in the Saudi Council of Ministers.

The Prince is a man of wealth, intellect, and bureaucratic skill with close family ties to the Royal family. A life of affluence, privilege, and power has allowed him to indulge in his more Satyr-ical side: the legendary half man, half goat with the permanent erection. He is exactly the wrong man to be entrusted with billions of dollars of the King's money, which makes him the perfect target for Mossad's Counter Threat Unit.

The CTU created a series of social networking accounts for Santi Joshi, AKA Rita Daveed, a freelance Indian journalist on assignment for the London Evening News profiling men and woman of power and influence. Her target is Prince Fahed. A spear phishing email was sent to Prince Fahed's office asking for an interview for the London Evening News' *Special Report on Men of Power and Influence*. These requests are normally, instantly deleted, but when Fahed's male assistant saw a photograph of the beautiful Santi Joshi hobnobbing with London bankers, he decided to forward the request on to the Prince. As soon as Fahed took one look at the photo, he clicked reply, thereby installing PupyRAT malware on his system, and simultaneously allowing the CTU to gain access to his computer and to every computer in the Saudi Department of Finance.

It seems the Prince has been investing in certain business opportunities that where in fact shell companies run by Iranian Intelligence for the purpose of funneling funds to certain terrorist groups that were enemies of both Israel and Saudi Arabia. If the information every got out, Prince or no Prince, Fahed would be toast. Fahed had no idea he was vulnerable, and his only current interest is in getting the luscious Santi Joshi into bed.

Fahed enters The Fumoir bar with his bodyguard. He spots Rita sitting at the bar sipping her cappuccino and nibbling on a macaroon. The Prince is a handsome, forty something man, with a well-trimmed beard, wearing an extravagantly expensive Savile Row suit. He takes the stool beside Rita, kisses her on the cheek and places his hand on her thigh. She gently removes it. Fahed orders a vodka martini.

Fahed: "Would you like a real drink or should we go right up stairs. I've taken the liberty of renting the King's Suite?"

Rita ignores the question. "I have something for you." She slides a brown, nine-by-twelve envelope across the bar in front of Fahed.

Fahed: "Is this the article?"

Rita: "Not exactly. Take a look."

Fahed slips the stack of papers out of the envelope. He glances at the page on top. His eyes go wide. He shuffles through the rest of the papers. He turns toward his bodyguard and starts to signal him.

Rita: "I wouldn't do that if I was you. Best you look around first."

Fahed waves off his man. He looks around. There's a couple sitting in the corner. They look directly at Fahed and smile. Fahed spots the bulge in the man's jacket. The woman reaches for her purse as if she is searching for her lipstick when in fact she is checking her Beretta. There's a man sitting at the other end of the bar who seems intent on discovering what's at the bottom of his whiskey sour. He looks up at Fahed and winks. There is another man and woman sitting in the other corner of the bar having a quiet conversation. They also seem to be well equipped. Fahed looks at Rita.

Rita: "Friends. I have lots of friends. And you'd be surprised where they pop up."

Fahed: "You're Mossad?"

Rita: "Who and what I am is irrelevant. The issue is simple. You came here to get laid, and instead you're getting fucked. It's as simple as that my dear."

Fahed sighs a knowing sigh. "So what do you want, money?"

Rita laughs, "No my dear, I don't want your money. All I want is your co-operation."

Fahed: "For what?"

Rita: "Your cousin Prince Abdullah is Deputy to the Foreign Minister. We want you to convince him to get the Minister to vote against that resolution in the UN next week."

Fahed: "Are you kidding? There's no way they'll do that, no matter what I tell them."

Rita: "Tell them it's a matter of national security. Convince them, or that report will be on CNN ten minutes after the vote."

Fahed runs his hand across his bearded chin. He looks at Rita. The lust has been replaced by desperation. "I think I can get them to abstain. That's the best I can do, really, if I can do that, it will be something."

Rita doesn't answer immediately. She knew from the beginning that getting the Saudis to abstain from the vote was the realistic prize, but Fahed doesn't have to know that.

Fahed: "Sati, or whatever the hell your name is, abstaining is the best I can do."

Rita gets as much satisfaction from the desperation in his voice than in the actual victory. In truth the Israelis don't give a shit about the vote. Everyone understands where everyone else stands. It's simply a matter of public perception. The real victory is in letting these assholes know they are vulnerable, and if they don't play ball, they can be fucked. "Okay, my dear, I think I can convince my people that abstaining will suffice."

Fahed: "What about this information, will you destroy it?"

Rita laughs again. "Don't be a fool Fahed. That report is just the tip of the iceberg. We've got enough dope on you and your people to have the whole department lined up in front of a firing squad or whatever you do to traitors these days."

Fahed: "I'm going to fucking kill you."

Rita finishes the last of her cappuccino. She pushes herself off the stool: "You can try, my dear." Fahed watches as she leaves. He'd still like to fuck her.

1
RATI DEVI
THE GODDESS OF SEX

Present Day

Rati Devi watches from behind the blacked-out windows of the Mercedes limousine as Tyler Raines steps out from the Siniestro City Council building into the California sunshine. Raines is a shabby little man of undistinguished talent and appearance. His clothes, no matter how expensive, always look like they are in dire need of a dry cleaner and an extra pass through a mangle clothes press. The middle-aged Raines is a short, bald, roly-poly lawyer of modest ability. What he does have going for him is he's the only lawyer in Siniestro, California. One would think that his marriage to the daughter of long-time mayor, the Honorable Malcolm C. Barnes, would be an advantage, but Mayor Barnes is not a fan. So it is no surprise that the Mayor convinced the governing council to turn down Raines' application for building permits for the new owners of the old Millbrook property: something about population density and maintaining the unique wine-country character of the Siniestro region.

In point of fact, Mayor Barnes and the other members of the consolidated city-county council wished to purchase Millbrook Estates and Winery for themselves and were very displeased when an outsider swooped in and paid old-man Millbrook a premium for the desirable property. To make matters worse, it's rumoured the new owners are some foreign hippy outfit that wanted to turn the place into a commune with a vodka distillery.

Raines drops his briefcase as he stumbles over the patterned concrete walkway that leads down to the street where Rati's limo is parked. The back window of the Mercedes rolls down revealing the mesmerizingly beautiful and exotic Rati Devi. Raines is out of breath from the short walk from the City Council steps to the limo, "I'm afraid we lost Miss Devi. The vote was five to zero." Although her face is passive, without expression, the vermillion *bindi* on her forehead seems to burn a whole in Raine's soul. She says nothing. The window of the limo rolls up leaving Tyler Raines standing in the middle of the street mopping his brow with a linen handkerchief. Rati taps her driver on the shoulder and the limo drives away.

Rati Devi is an unusual woman, born Rita Daveed in Jerusalem she spent her early years like any other Israeli youngster. She went to Tel Aviv University where she studied psychology and marketing. After graduating and serving in the army with distinction she decided to follow her roots and take an extended vacation to India where her grandparents were born and raised. Her *bubbie* and *zadie* emigrated from Kochi, a major port city on the south-west coast of India bordering the Laccadive Sea shortly after Israel became a state in 1948.

According to *Zadie* Daveed the family are descendents of the Cochin Jews, teak, ivory and spice traders from Judea that arrived in Cochin around 562 BCE and decided to settle and make India their home.

During Rita's pilgrimage to India she ran out of money. She heard about a Hindu mystic, Baba Bhang, that was looking for someone to run his expanding *ashram* while he devoted himself to the principles of *Charvaka*. It didn't take long for Rita to learn *Bhang* is cannabis and the adherents of Baba Bhang's version of *Charvaka* believe that one's life should be devoted to the pursuit of pleasure enhanced by the consumption of large quantities of Bhang Lassi, a marijuana milkshake.

Charvakas believe that life on earth is all there is, so make the best of it with an energetic pursuit of the most delicious foods, the finest silks, and sublime sex. Of course, Bhang, the favorite treat of the Lord Shiva, is a particularly fine way to extract the most pleasure out of each sensual experience. It's not surprising adherents of Baba Bhang's over-the-top version of spiritual awakening were lining up for whatever cool aid the goofy guru was selling. When Rita showed up for the interview, Baba Bhang took one look at her and hired her on the spot, renaming her Rati Devi, the goddess of love, passion, and sexual pleasure.

With Rati's help word spread to the United States about Baba Bhang's approach to temporal happiness. As interest grew, Rati decided it was time to bring enlightenment to the home of the brave and the land of the free. It's not that she believed any of this horseshit, she was still Rita Daveed at heart, but as far as the followers of Baba Bhang were concerned she was Rati Devi, and it paid very handsomely to be the goddess of carnal pleasure, especially since she held a fifty percent share of Baba Bhang Corporation.

2

ARTIE PEARL
THE AMBULANCE CHASER

Artie Pearl looks at the ancient Jewish couple sitting across his impressive walnut partner's desk. The desk may be called a partner's desk, but he's not a partner, not even close. The desk is just a prop, an expensive staging device designed to inspire confidence, where none is deserved. It isn't that Artie is immune to the troubles of others; it just isn't part of his job description. Artie's only actual function at Levi, Washington, and Chan is to extract retainers from naïve potential clients that think the answer to their problems is to hire a smart Jewish lawyer.

This afternoon's victim is a pair of octogenarian retirees that were in a car accident. The elderly woman looks at her husband with concern in her eyes and says something in Yiddish. Artie smiles, gets up, and comes around to the client side of the desk. He squats down on his haunches in his custom-made suit so he is eye-to-eye with the old lady. Show respect and deference; always be polite; and act like you're a concerned grandson.

He touches the woman's hand like he's consoling his aged *bubbie*: "Mrs Garfield, we're not all shysters." He reaches for the documents on his desk, pulls out a hidden wooden extension and places the papers along with his Mont Blanc *Rouge et Noir* on top. "I look at you Mrs. Garfield, and I see my *own bubbie, Bubbie Zissel, alav ha-shalom*." The reference to his deceased grandmother and the Yiddish are nice touches. Artie knows just how to play it, but his real *bubbie* is alive and well, playing the nickel slots at Circus, Circus.

"Why don't I leave you two alone for a few minutes so you can make up your minds. I only want what's best for you and Sam, but if you think I'm only in it for the money, then please… don't sign." He leaves room. He'll give them just enough time to convince themselves of what he knows they've already decided; it won't take long, he knows he's won, the deal is done. *Bubbie Zissel, alav ha-shalom* is the closing pitch, and it rarely fails to work.

Arthur S. Pearl is an LA lawyer; not a particularly good lawyer, but a lawyer nonetheless. A close look at his resume would alert you to his educational qualifications. Oh he has a law degree alright, from Tourbillion University, the evidence of which, an ornate gold embossed parchment, hangs prominently on his office wall in an expensive frame that is far more impressive than the education he received. Tourbillion University's law school is ranked consistently by the ABA in the bottom ten percent of law schools that still manage to hold on to their accreditation, and Artie graduated nowhere near the top of his class.

Artie is no dummy, in fact, he is quite clever, but hard work was never really his thing. As such, he wound-up at Tourbillion, rather than Harvard or Yale or some other ivory covered institution specializing in producing a higher order of conmen than those spewed forth from the loins of good old TU. Most of his time at school was spent surfing on the beaches of Carpinteria. And so, instead of working for some prestigious law firm that dealt with business bigwigs, media titans, and entertainment elites, he worked for Levi, Washington, and Chan, whose claim to fame are their ethically challenged, ethnically centered late night infomercials featuring Morris Levi, Jakobe Washington, and Kingston Chan, each with their own distinct target market sales pitch.

Artie does have several qualities that make him the perfect asset for a firm like Levi, Washington, and Chan. He is handsome, likeable, charming, and Jewish. His one great skill is his ability to convince just about anybody that he is on their side and that he would do anything in his power to help them get what they want, or what they think they deserve. In the case of Mr. and Mrs. Garfield, they signed the retainer agreement and a check, just like Artie knew they would, and that would be the last time the elderly couple would ever see Artie Pearl. The case would be handed off to some unpleasant grunt who would churn the account until the Garfield's ran out of cash or got completely fed up.

3

BABA BHANG
THE GURU

Artie sits at his desk mulling over where he should go for dinner. His secretary buzzes. A new potential client has arrived. He tells his secretary to show them in. He stands to greet them. When the door opens Artie is surprised, no *bubbie* and *zadie* this time, it must be a mistake.

Standing in front of him is an antediluvian character with skin the color and texture of dried roasted walnuts; he's wearing a saffron silk robe and matching baggy pyjama-style trousers. The colorful outfit reminds Artie of the pictures he's seen of the Holi celebration where Indians celebrate by tossing colored powder on one another while spraying each other with special water guns called *pichkaris*. Around his neck is a strand of dark *rudraksha* beads called a *mala*. His hair and full beard is a mixture of black, gray, and white, and explodes off his head like it was styled by Albert Einstein's hairdresser.

With him is a woman of magical beauty. She wears a charcoal gray custom-tailored man's suit of wool and mohair and a black cashmere turtleneck sweater. The male-inspired getup doesn't hide the perfectly proportioned body that hugs the goat and wool fibres. Her hair is long and black; it glistens like its has been lit by George Hurrell himself. The only manifestation of her Indian heritage is the red *bindi* of vermillion powder that sits above the bridge of her perfectly shaped nose. She is the most exquisite creature Artie Pearl has ever seen, and he wants her, and not just as a client. She smiles a knowing smile; she knows she has that effect on men. She touches his hand as if to bring him back to reality, "May we sit?"

Artie starts to regain his shattered composure. "Yes, yes, of course, but are you sure you're here to see me?"

She points to the diploma on the wall. "You are Arthur S. Pearl, aren't you?"

His eyes follow her long delicate finger as if it is a magic wand. He looks at his diploma and sees his name in some ornate gold embossed font. "Yes I'm Arthur Pearl, but everyone just calls me Artie, it's more friendly." He knows he sounds like an idiot.

She sits in one of the fabric covered chairs across from Artie's desk. Her colourful companion sits in the chair beside her. She looks up at Artie and smiles once more. "Well Artie, according to that fancy diploma on your wall, you're a lawyer. You are a lawyer aren't you Artie?"

Artie moves behind his desk and sits, doing his best to act professionally, "Yes of course."

She unbuttons her suit jacket giving Artie a better view of her perfectly formed breasts as they strain against the cashmere fabric and the black leather shoulder holster that holds her Glock 26 Sub-Compact Semi Automatic. "Well Artie my love, we need a lawyer."

If Artie was transfixed before, now he is stunned. Her words spar for attention with the fleeting glimpse of the firearm. Self-preservation wins out. "I think there's been a mistake, I'm a personal injury lawyer, not a criminal layer."

She points to the diploma on the wall one more time. "That piece of parchment says Arthur S. Pearl is a licensed lawyer in the State of California and you've told us that you are Arthur S. Pearl, whose friends and clients call Artie, because it's more friendly. So Artie my love, we want to hire you as our representative." She reaches into her pocket and takes out a check and places it on Artie's desk. The check is for fifty thousand dollars and it's made out to Arthur S. Pearl not Levi, Washington, and Chan.

Artie looks at the check, then at the Hindu mystic that still hasn't said a word, and then at the woman. "This check is made out to me, not the firm." He looks down at the check one more time and sees it has been signed by Rati Devi, Chief Executive Officer of Baba Bhang Corporation. "Who's Rati Devi?"

The woman smiles, "I am Rati and this…" she nods toward her colourful companion, "is Baba Bhang." The guru smiles a goofy smile while his head wobbles on top of his neck like a Jose Bautista bobble head. "Perhaps I should explain. We've purchased a vineyard and a large plot of land in Siniestro Country. We want to expand and in order to do that we need followers and more production space for our new distillery. The disciples will need somewhere to stay, so we need building permits, but the good people of Siniestro County have repeatedly denied our applications."

Artie runs his hand over his chin, "And why would they do that?"

Rati: "They're prejudice and parochial. The locals don't like people like us; people who don't look like them, dress like them, or pray like them. You see, we are a spiritual order. Baba Bhang is a Guru, a Hindu mystic and teacher who guides our order and teaches our followers the principles of *Charvaka*. We operate a winery in order to raise funds and we have plans to add a vodka distillery. We are no different from the Christian monks that used to operate wineries. The check is made out to you because we want you to work for us exclusively and the check is your first month's salary. Of course you can bill us for expenses. Does that answer all your questions, Artie my love."

Artie: "Just one more. Why me? I'm just a second rate ambulance chaser."

Rati: "Do you know anything about pearls, Artie my love?" Artie shakes his head. "A pearl starts off as an irritating foreign object that finds its way into a special mollusk where it is surrounded and layered with a protective coating until it becomes a lustrous finely colored gem. You, Artie my love, are that irritating foreign object, and we are the welcoming protective mollusk that will turn you into a lustrous finely colored gem. And we'll pay you six hundred thousand dollars a year to start."

Artie looks at Baba Bhang who smiles his goofy smile while his head wobbles on top of his neck. Artie looks at Rati, who he would eventually find out is named after the Hindu goddess of lust; and that's not the only surprise Artie would find out about his new employer.

4

THE HINDQUARTER

The consolidated county-city of Siniestro looks like something plucked out of a Disney theme park dedicated to Hans Christian Andersen. Its main street, Copenhagen Boulevard, consists of two rows of quaint two and three-story brightly colored buildings trimmed with decorative wood panels and flower boxes. The planters overflow with blooms of every shape, color, and variety, including some that look like they were lifted out of one of Van Gogh's masterpieces, except Van Gogh was Dutch not Danish, but this is America where cultural absurdity is a way of life.

The area was settled by Danish farmers prior to the turn of the century, the twentieth, not the twenty-first. Today the county calls twenty-five hundred and-thirty-three inhabitants spread throughout the town and the surrounding vineyards home. The wineries and the caricature Danish simulation are the main drawing cards attracting wine snobs eager to taste the local vintages and families with snot-nosed kids whose parents calculate the fake Danish experience is cheaper than a trip to the real thing.

One end of Copenhagen Boulevard is dominated by a faux windmill that advertises itself as the place to go for original Danish cuisine. Jepsen House features quasi Danish originals like *Frikadeller* (two large pork meatballs with boiled potatoes and vegetables) or *Krebinetter* (two oval-shaped pork patties with boiled potatoes and vegetables); and for the kids there's *Rodpolse* (an extra long red-dyed hot dog covered in mustard, ketchup mayonnaise, pickles and raw onions served on a baguette along with boiled potatoes and vegetables). There are other things on the menu but be assured, they all come with boiled potatoes and vegetables. The Jepsen wind-milled eatery fronts the pseudo Danish décor of the Jepsen Hotel owned by Carol Jepsen.

If imitation Danish dining doesn't tickle your taste buds, you can take the twelve and a half minute stroll to the other end of town where you will find Carol Jepsen's competition, the Hindquarter Inn, a mocha-yellow and brown half-timbered hotel that houses the Garrison Grill, serving centered-cut top sirloin steaks with fully loaded baked potatoes or grilled chicken with sweet potato fries; and your choice of homemade chocolate chiffon pie or coconut cream cake for dessert.

The Hindquarter Inn features a more modern and vastly more authentic interior design aesthetic with Arne Jacobsen Egg Chairs in the lounge and AJ Cutlery adding style and elegance to the crisp white linen that adorns the Garrison tables lit by Cecilie Manz's Caravaggio Lamps. When a guest arrives expecting a more gingerbread version of Danish culture, they are offered a complimentary Carlsberg to ease their disappointment. The owner of the Hindquarter Inn is Erik Garrison, an ex jockey that inherited the hostelry from his parents who ran the establishment for years. Garrison also inherited a small ranch next to the Millbrook Winery where he trains the occasional thoroughbred for some of his old racing cronies.

When Artie Pearl, Baba Bhang's new lawyer arrived in town, Rati had him installed in a suite on the top floor of the Hindquarter Inn, right next to her room. For the time being, his arrival went unnoticed as the town was enjoying a banner tourist season. That anonymity would not last.

5
MAKING FRIENDS WITH THE NATIVES

Artie Pearl isn't a cynic; he doesn't see everything and everybody in varying shades of black; he's more of a charcoal gray sort of guy. He understands America is not, and never has been, a melting pot of diversity and tolerance as so eloquently expressed in Emma Lazarus's poem carved into the plaque on the base of the Statue of Liberty. It's not that America is so different from other parts of the world, it only thinks it is. The fact is Southerners still detest Northerners for winning the Civil War more than a hundred and fifty years after it ended; East Coasters still think West Coasters are flakes even though the colorful chaos of Haight Ashbury has long since disappeared from the rear-view mirror; and we won't even raise the ugly spectre of segregation, animosity, and fear that exists between the religious, ethnic, and hyphenated inhabitants of the home of the brave and the land of the free. No, Artie Pearl is a realist. He knows Armani and overalls don't play nicely with one another; as such, his first order of business before he even gets settled in his new home at the Hindquarter Inn is to visit the offices of Tyler Raines, Esquire, Attorney-at-Law.

The office Tyler Raines is located on the second floor of a two-story, red-roofed, yellow stucco building with red painted timbers in alternating rows of perfect squares and criss-crosses. Matching red awnings protect the tourists that browse the pastries in the window of Frieda's Danish Delights located on the first floor of Raines' building.

Tyler's law practice consists mostly of mundane matters like wills and real estate deals. There just isn't a lot of anything else in Siniestro that requires a lawyer. Lately there's been some heated real estate disputes, but that usually involves outsiders like Rati Devi coming into the county wanting to buy vineyards and turn them into housing developments.

There is little Mayor Barnes and his council can do about locals selling to outsiders, but when those outsiders come to the council for building permits, they find their applications summarily rejected.

After several unsuccessful attempts at obtaining building permits, the interlopers eventually give-up and accept a lowball offer from a local citizen, usually one that sits on the council with Mayor Barnes. In point of fact, Raines' father-in-law, Mayor Barnes, and his council *compadres* have amassed quite a nice parcel of properties that they rent to rich Angelinos that think owning a vineyard and having your name on a bottle of chardonnay is as classy as it gets.

Artie Pearl sits across from the chubby lawyer listening carefully to all the excuses and reasons why Baba Bhang Corporation's application for building permits were turned down.

Raines: "I'm sorry Miss Devi dragged you out here, Mr. Pearl, but there's little I can do to help. Miss Devi has been very generous, but I did warn her that her application would be rejected. People think because I'm married to the Mayor's daughter that I have some kind of inside track in getting things done, but if truth be told, the son-of-a-bitch hates me; and I'm not so sure his daughter doesn't feel the same. For the right price I'd ask you to put in a good word with..." he picks up Artie's card from his desk and looks at it, "Levi, Washington, and Chan. I'll tell you straight out Mr. Pearl, this fake Danish tourist trap might look like a city boy's wet dream, but all it delivers is blanks."

Artie smiles, "I get it, Tyler, I really do… you don't mind if I call you Tyler do you?" Raines smiles a broad smile like he's just been invited into the big boys' club. Artie's charm offensive is working.

Raines takes the bait, "No, please do, my friends call me Ty."

Artie returns the smile, "And please, Mr. Pearl is my father, call me Artie." If Raines' chest puffed out any more Artie might get injured by a flying plastic button from Raines' non-iron Brooks Brothers' shirt. "Here's the thing Ty, I'm stuck here just like you. I don't work for Levi, Washington, and Chan anymore. I work exclusively for BBE LLC.

Raines: "Who are they?"

Artie: "BBE is the holding company that owns Baba Bhang Corporation. Between you and me, Ty, I figured Baba Bhang sounded a little too ethnic to be accepted by the locals." Raines nods in agreement. Artie continues, "So before I came to your charming wine country paradise, I set up BBE."

Tyler: "Smart move. I would have done the same thing."

Artie: "Also, I did a little checking and you are spot-on with your analysis of the situation, but have you ever wondered where your wife's father and his friends get the dough to buy all these properties?"

Raines leans forward as if Artie is about to tell him where to find the Ark of the Covenant. "I never thought about it. They're leaders of the community and they all have big spreads and fancy wine operations. I just figured they had the cash."

Artie: "Sure these guys got assets, but they're mortgaged to the hilt. There's no way they can plunk down the kind of dough they've been shelling out. They got to have some sugar daddy hiding in the bushes. And if they do, there must be more to this real estate Peyton Place than protecting grapes and maintaining imitation cultural purity."

Raines leans so hard against his desk in an attempt to get closer to Artie that he almost spills his coffee. "You think some big developer from LA or back East has something going with the Council?"

Artie sits back in his chair like he's exhausted from revealing his surprise conspiracy theory. He shrugs. "I don't know Ty, that's why I need your help." The whale has been harpooned, now all Artie has to do is get him onboard.

Raines: "You want my help, you got it. Those assholes, including my wife's father, have never given me the time of day. You'd think they would throw some business my way, maybe even get me involved in their deals, not that I would you understand, but still, I am married to the guy's daughter, and she's always bitching to Daddy that I don't make enough money. The hell with them. What do you need me to do?"

The whale's onboard. Phase one is about to begin. Artie reaches into his Armani jacket and takes out a check. He hands it to Raines. Tyler's eyes go wide, "Who do I have to kill to earn this?"

Artie: "For now… nobody." Raines is a bit surprised by the vague response.

Raines: "I was just…"

Artie: "... kidding. I know. All you have to do right now is find out who's financing the county fathers' real estate purchases. I'm staying at the Hindquarter. Everybody thinks I'm just a tourist, so let's keep it our little secret." Raines runs a finger across his lips signifying mum's the word.

Artie searches his jacket pocket for a card. He finds what he's looking for and hands it to Raines. "Next time you're in LA, go see my friend, Mo Fields. He's the best tailor on the West Coast; by the time he's finished with you, George Clooney will be calling you for sartorial advice. You work for me now, and I want you to look the part."

6
THE HIDDEN TREASURE

Whoever was financing the land purchases had an agenda, mostly likely it was a housing development play, but Artie had a suspicion there was more to it than just housing. While Raines pursued the byzantine ownership paper trail of recent Siniestro land purchases, Artie went back to LA to cleanup a few personal odds and ends. While in town he stopped by the Three Kings Bespoke Tailor Shop to say hello to his pal Mo Fields to order a couple of suits and warn him of the pending visit from Siniestro's portly village advocate. Artie told Mo about his new job in Siniestro and was surprised to hear that Mo was a friend of Erik Garrison. Artie knew most of the executives that worked at the Hancock Entertainment Complex got their suits made at The Three Kings. Part of the complex included a racetrack, so it wasn't surprising that Mo knew Erik Garrison, owner of the Hindquarter Inn. Mo offered to call Garrison to put in a good word. Like most jockeys, Garrison is small and tough, with a take no prisoners attitude under his polished innkeeper exterior. He just might be the kind of friend that could come in handy if things got sticky. Artie's strategy of co-opting friendly locals was starting to take shape.

On his way back to Siniestro he decided to pay a visit to the Carpinteria Retirement Village; the new home of Mort Millbrook, eighty-seven-year-old former owner of the Millbrook Winery and Estates. Millbrook was a nice old gent that welcomed the young visitor and was happy to discuss his land sale over a bottle of Millbrook Sauvignon Blanc, a delightful drink with traces of green apple, sour pear, grapefruit and lemon that tickles the tongue as it goes down, at least, that's the way the old man described the prized remnant of his life's work.

Millbrook rambled on for half-an-hour telling stories of the good old days, how he and a few brave friends did the dirty work in building California's wine reputation.

He wasn't a fan of the celebrity wine snobs that bought out small wineries just so they could slap their name on a bottle to impress their friends. He had even less regard for the developers who were willing to rip up his life's work in order to slap together a bunch of badly constructed imitation Spanish villas. At least the wine dilettantes kept the wineries operating and weren't interested in ticky-tacky housing developments, or even worse, drill for oil… at which point Artie almost chocked on the Sauvignon.

Artie: "Did you say oil?"

Millbrook: "God damn right, I said oil, son. Every few years some carpetbagger comes along with some old yellowing geological report that claims there's oil in Siniestro County. Got to do the fracking to get it out. Well fuck them. I don't want them ugly oil wells all over my land. I don't need the dough, and my kids are all big shots in Hollywood. They got more money than God. I rather sell my land to that pretty Indian girl with the crackpot guru… you should see this guy, doesn't say much but his head wobbles and bobbles like its screws need tightening."

Artie sat and listened as Mort Millbrook went on for another fifteen minutes about how the pretty Indian woman got his dried-up juices flowing one last time and how he preferred to sell his land to her and the goofy guru because they were going to keep the winery operating. Artie stopped listening when he heard the word oil. Now he knows the why, all he had to do was find the who.

7
AN ALTERNATIVE PLAN

While Artie is in LA, Rati busies herself reorganizing things at the winery. The entrance to the property is guarded by two stone pillars, one with a painted weathered sign that used to announce you'd arrived at "Millbrook Winery and Estates." Old man Millbrook wouldn't be happy to see the sign replaced with a new one that read, "The Baba Bhang Center, Home of The Baba Bhang Winery and Distillery and The Baba Bhang Meditation Retreat." The distillery and retreat were perhaps, wishful thinking, as the Siniestro County Council seemed determined to obstruct whatever plans the goofy guru and his lovely sidekick had planned.

The addition of a meditation retreat complete with a hotel is a natural extension needed to accommodate visiting followers of the 'Maharishi of Exquisite Pleasure' as the local newspaper, The Siniestro Sun, announced in bold headline type. The Editor of the paper, Sam Neil, along with other members of the Siniestro Merchants Association were not all fans of the Council's hegemonic approach to local Siniestro purity.

These local entrepreneurs welcomed the oddball newcomers as they promised an influx of new visitors who would need the services and amenities of the local businesses. The town merchants were leery of the Council's restrictive policies but had no evidence of any nefarious intent. The Council did have the backing of the rival and influential Siniestro Wine Owners Association whose position was the county's prosperity depended on its wine country reputation and anything that interfered or competed with that local image was detrimental to the community writ large.

The newly dubbed Baba Bhang Winery is a natural money-maker for a cult that believes in the somewhat corrupted *Charvaka* philosophy of wine, women, and wanton pleasure, but a distillery? On the surface it seems like an odd add-on, but in fact, it is not. Bhang infused vodka and rum are reliable weed consumables with tried-and-true recipes, despite the inherent dangers of overindulging in potent hallucinogens. They are metaphysical catalysts for adventurist adherents, willing to risk a more intoxicating transcendental experience, not to mention the potential physiological and mental dangers of too much of two good things, weed and booze. For teetotalers that want the Bhang without the added kick of hard spirits, there is Bhang Lassi, a cannabis milkshake that by itself is able to provide an enhanced existential awakening.

There are several existing buildings already in-place on the estate to accommodate the winery, warehouse, and a large souvenir shop where guests can sample the liquid merchandise and buy branded t-shirts, windbreakers, and ball caps. There is a large hacienda style mansion that currently serves as the living quarters for Baba Bhang and his three mistresses as well as the offices of the winery and the newly formed BBE, LLC.

The expansion plans for the property include the distillery, the meditation retreat, and a hotel. These plans were drawn up by a Mumbai architect, a follower of Baba Bhang. When Artie saw the design sketches, he couldn't help but smile. The Indian draftsman had incorporated a series of freestanding x-rated monuments depicting the erotic sculptures of the Khajuraho temples. Artie suggested that a local designer with knowledge of regional sensibilities might be easier for the Council to accept, but of course, that was before Artie knew about the hidden agenda and the real reason for the repeated rejections.

Rati is nothing if not determined in her imaginative response to the Council's attempts to block the expansion. This is California after all, where the weather is beautiful and there's a general acceptance of all things bizarre, especially if they promise a path to spiritual enlightenment through unbridled pleasure enhanced by a liquid potion of Mary Jane.

As an interim measure, Rati had a local company set up a large circus-sized tent able to accommodate almost one hundred followers surrounded by twenty-five smaller tents each able to sleep four adults. Emails were sent to Baba's American followers announcing the opening of the tent city and a series of lectures by the Guru of Pleasure himself, the human bobble head, Baba Bhang. The three day lecture series cost forty-five hundred dollars, but it includes an unlimited supply of Bhang Lassi and a Baba Bhang t-shirt and a hat that proudly announces. "I Bhanged With Baba."

When word of the tent city found its way back to Mayor Barnes and his Council; they were not happy. The Mayor and two of his colleagues decided to visit the renamed Millbrook property in order to deliver a cease and desist letter.

8
BABA'S TENT CITY

Old hippies, insecure Hollywood types, and artists searching for inspiration all arrive in Siniestro looking for whatever life promised when they were young and had somehow slipped away as time past. The invasion of pleasure seekers, enlightenment junkies, and weed weirdoes soon filled tent city with the overflow cramming into every available rental space Siniestro had to offer. Garrison's Hindquarter Inn is packed and the local restaurants and souvenir shops are breaking all kinds of sales records. The shopkeepers and business owners are ecstatic; the wannabe oil barons, not so much. When Artie arrives back in town, he heads out to the compound to report to Rati and set up his new office as Senior Vice President of BBE, LLC.

Mayor Barnes, two of his Council colleagues, and Sheriff Tomkins arrive at the gate of the Baba Bhang Center with a cease and desist letter in hand. They are greeted by two humorless ex-Shabak agents. During Rati's time in the Israeli army she was occasionally lent out to the Shabak, also known as the Shin Bet, and on occasion the Mossad as in the case of Prince Fahed. Israeli Security Agencies found Rati's hypnotic charms useful when setting up a honey trap.

The two ex security agents, friends of Rati, usher the three guests into an intimate boardroom in what used to be the office of old-man Millbrook. The two security men position themselves on either side of the entrance. An attractive Indian woman wearing a saffron and gold saree enters the room carrying a tray with six glasses and a bottle of Baba Bhang Vodka with a label designed by one of the leading psychedelic artists of the sixties.

The surprise visit by the Mayor and his cronies is in fact not a surprise at all. Barnes, figuring he was doing his Son-in-Law a favor went to Raines to issue the cease and desist letter, but Raines declined citing a conflict of interest. When Barnes asked what local client could possibly create a conflict of interest, Raines refused to answer. Barnes was furious. As soon as Barnes stomped out of Raines' office, Tyler picked up the phone and called Artie. An hour later Erik Garrison shows up at Raines' office with a check for a thousand dollars from the Siniestro Merchants Association. Garrison told Raines he received a call from Artie and he suggested Raines represent the Association in all matters relating to the merchants' collective interests. The battle for the future of Siniestro Country had begun.

Barnes can hardly contain his anger when he sees his Son-in-Law enter the boardroom all chummy with Rati and Artie. The look on the Mayor's face is almost worth as much as Artie's check. Raines smiles, "Hi Dad."

Barnes: "What the hell are you doing here?"

Raines: "I told you I couldn't represent you in this matter as I had a conflict of interest."

Barnes: "You represent these crazy hippies?"

Raines: "In fact, I do."

Barnes: "Since when?"

Raines: "Since Mr. Pearl gave me a fucking big retainer. I also represent the Siniestro Merchants' Association, whose interests coincide with that of The Baba Bhang Corporation and its parent holding company, BBE, LLC."

You can almost see the steam emanating from Mayor Barnes' ears, but he retains his cool as best he can. Barnes looks at Artie: "And who are you?"

Artie sticks out his hand obligating Barnes and his pals to shake it. "I'm Artie Pearl, in-house council and Senior Vice President of BBE and of course you already know Miss Devi, President of BBE."

Barnes: "Where's the sheik or whatever the hell you call him?"

Rati: "Gentlemen please sit so we can discuss this issue cordially like the community leaders I know you are." Despite their obvious belligerent intentions, the men can't help but physically wilt under the spell of the guru's strikingly beautiful muse. Barnes, his colleagues, and the Sheriff sit. Artie and Raines follow. Rati opens the bottle of Baba Bhang Vodka and pours hefty portions in each of the six glasses. She hands one glass to each man and keeps one for herself. "Gentlemen, please taste a sample of our new product. No matter what comes of today's meeting, at least we can all enjoy life's small pleasures together." Barnes and his men hesitate. Rati takes a delicate sip of the vodka, "Gentlemen, please, give it a try." The men all take a sip, and then a healthy gulp. Rati then tops up their glasses.

As Raines and Pearl individually review the cease and desist letter, Rati continues mesmerizing the visitors with the *Charvaka* philosophy of enjoying the here and now to its fullest, and as she does, she keeps refilling the men's glasses with more samples of the Baba's new product. The beautiful saree clad assistant arrives with more glasses and a new bottle with a different sixties' inspired psychedelic label, but this time the refreshment is Bhang infused rum.

The men can't take their eyes off of Rati and the beautiful assistant who continues refilling the three men's glasses while Rati, Artie, and Raines nurse their original drinks. There are several attempts to get to the point of the visit but they're frustrated by Raines's insistence that the bylaw used as an excuse to shut down the tent city only applies to the actual Village of Siniestro and not to the County as a whole. The Baba Bhang Center is located in Siniestro County but outside the actual city limits of the Village of Siniestro.

Before the discussion can deteriorate into a heated argument, more drinks are poured and more stories of the joys of *Charvaka* are extolled. Within an hour, the three guests are *baked* on Bhang-infused vodka and rum. They can barely contain their drooling over Rati and the pretty assistant. All efforts to discuss the shutting down of the tent city are abandoned. When the rum and vodka finally runs out, the civic leaders decide to leave. As they do, they run into Baba Bhang and his beautiful threesome.

The men giggle when the Baba's head swivels around his neck like an out-of-control gyroscope. They salivate over his three exotic companions and wonder how this bizarre character in the orange pyjamas could attract such extraordinary creatures. None of the group are in any condition to drive; they can barely negotiate the sidewalk leading to the parking area. As they travel back to town, they argue over which one of the beautiful ladies they'd like to bed.

According to the next day's Siniestro Sun, the Mayor, the Sheriff and a contingent of County Councillors were found in a ditch at the side of the road on the outskirts of the village. The men suffered various injuries, none of which were life-threatening, but severe none-the-less. According to sources at the Siniestro County Hospital, the men all had high levels of alcohol and cannabis in their systems. Since the Sheriff was among the group, it is unlikely anyone will be charged, but there are rumors that an Assistant States' Attorney is looking into the matter.

9

JORDAN SAINT-IVES
THE OIL SLICK

Every square inch of the circus tent that houses the temporary home of the Baba Bhang Meditation Center is occupied. The saffron Clarabell of Self Indulgence has just finished the first half of his rambling esoteric seminar on the *Charvaka* path to a hedonistic existence. The one hundred and twenty-six standing-room only adherents have been captivated and transfixed by the human bobble head's every word; at forty-five hundred dollars a pop, that's the least he could do.

Jordan Saint-Ives stands at the back of the tent fascinated by the sociological manipulation he's just witnessed. The psychology is simple: everyone desires pleasure, that's a given. What the Baba offers is cultural permission, a release from the Judeo-Christian restrictions, admonishments, and threats of eternal damnation. This is freedom to pursue desire without guilt. As far as cults go, this one has an irresistible hook. What took an hour of almost indecipherable bafflegab could be summed up in one simple aphorism: "eat, drink, and screw, because tomorrow you're fucked," a crass but effective message.

Jordan Saint-Ives, real name Avrum Lipinsky, is sixty-years-old but looks like he's in his late forties. He has a shock of salt and pepper hair styled with just enough disarray to give him an air of someone in the arts, perhaps a movie director or producer. In fact Avrum Lipinsky is an arranger, not of music, but of deals, international deals between parties that are nominally enemies, but as is often the case in international affairs, enemies make strange bedfellows. The kids have a word for it, frenemies, but in Lipinsky's world, frenemies are more like Tupac and Biggie with nukes, rather than Swift and Kardashian with tweets.

Saint-Ives wanders out into the California sun as saree clad beauties hand out cardboard cups of Bhang Lassi to the faithful. Saint-Ives makes his way to the hacienda offices where he is intercepted by the two ex-Shabak agents. The guards are polite but purposefully intimidating. Saint-Ives recognizes the type: their guttural accents and nonchalant dismissive attitude indicates ex-Israeli intelligence, either Shin Bet or Mossad. The senior of the two steps forward blocking Saint-Ives from entering, "Can we help you Sir?"

Saint-Ives: "Tell Rita, Avrum wants to see her." The security man's nonchalant manner disappears in an instant. The senior guard snaps his fingers and the second man comes forward and pats Saint-Ives down. "I'm not carrying, now tell Daveed I'm here, עַכְשָׁיו! (*ahkh-shahv*). The senior security man nods to his partner who disappears into the back office. A few minutes later Rati and Artie come out. Saint-Ives goes to greet Rati but the bodyguard steps in front blocking his way.

Rati: "It's okay Joseph, the gentleman is an old friend." The guard steps aside.

Saint-Ives kisses Rati on the cheek. He looks at Artie and sticks out his hand for him to shake. "This your new boyfriend?"

Rati doesn't answer. "Funny, I didn't see your name on the guest list." Saint-Ives reaches into his pocket and hands Rati his card: "*Jordan Saint-Ives, Consultant, Canary Wharf, London, England.*" Rati smiles, "Saint-Ives, how every *goysha*. Why don't we go for a walk, I've been stuck in meetings all day?" The two security men follow as Rati takes the lead with Artie on one side and Saint-

Ives on the other. "What do you want, Avrum? I know you're not here for the spiritual guidance"

Saint-Ives: "It appears you've accidentally wandered into the middle of something. When I heard you were involved, I convinced Management that you would be amenable to co-operate at the right price, but only if it came from the right person."

Artie: "And you're that person?"

Saint-Ives: "Yes Mr. Pearl, I am."

Rati: "Just as a matter of interest, what do consider the right price?"

Saint-Ives: "Twenty million for the property and five million each to you and Mr. Pearl for... let's call it, consultant fees."

Rati: "That sounds like a very generous offer." As she continues walking she turns to Artie, "What do you think my love?"

Artie's has grown accustom to Rati's habit of calling him 'my love,' a familiarity that has been solidified by late night knocks on his Hindquarter door. Nevertheless, his faces goes pink, "Why not fifty, ten, and ten? Anyone willing to offer that kind of dough for this winery must think there's pirate treasure buried on the property."

Saint-Ives: "Let's not be coy Mr. Pearl, we all know what's buried under the property, and as far as the offer is concerned, twenty, five, and five is just an opening bid, but my employers do have their limits. Fifty, ten, and ten might be acceptable, but understand, to them it's all just numbers on a ledger. If the debits for war add up to less than those for peace, then war it is."

As they return to the entrance of the hacienda, Rati turns to Saint-Ives, "That sounds an awful lot like a threat, Avrum."

Saint-Ives: "I'm just the messenger Rita, you know that. I wouldn't want to see anything bad happen to you or lover boy; I know how protective you get of your pets." Artie ignores the taunt.

Saint-Ives: "These people play hardball. Take the money and run. This whole hippie scam you got going will eventually blow up in your face. Get out while you can. Five, maybe ten million, is nothing to sneeze at. Isn't that right Mr. Pearl?"

Rati turns to Artie, "What do you think my love?"

Artie: "The smart thing to do is take the money, but if there's oil, this place is worth a lot more than what your friend is offering."

Saint-Ives: "There are no guarantees in the oil business. This whole play could be a dud, or just too costly to pursue. Like I said, it's all about the debits and the credits, but make no mistake, they're prepared to fight."

Rati: "I don't like to be threatened and I'm inclined to turn down your offer."

Saint-Ives: "That would be a mistake."

Artie touches Rati's hand: "We have options, if you want."

Rati: "Well Arum my old friend, there it is. I'm afraid we're not interested in your offer."

Saint-Ives shrugs, "I made the pitch. I'll pass on your answer." He kisses Rati on the cheek, one last time, "By the way, Prince Fahed sends his love. He told me to tell you, no hard feelings and you're welcome back anytime."

Rati laughs: "I'm afraid a public beheading is not on my to do list. Tell him to go fuck himself and if he sends any of his flunkies after me, remind him I still have dangerous friends." Saint-Ives nods and heads towards the parking lot. Rati and Artie watch as he gets into his car for the drive back to LA.

As Saint-Ives pulls onto the highway, he presses the phone button on the steering wheel of his Aston Martin DB11. "It's a no, but the lawyer floated a counter offer: fifty, ten and ten… They know about the oil. Maybe we underestimated this guy's ability… I told you, Rita is off limits, untouchable. Fuck with her and I'm not the only one you'll have to deal with. Just remember, she's got friends in Glilot Junction… The lawyer? I guess so, but I wouldn't advise it. The two of them got something going. I know Rita, she doesn't like people messing with her toys… Okay, if that's what you want, but you're going to really piss her off… Yah, yah.. I heard you. I'll get it done."

10
"KILL ALL THE LAWYERS"
- Dick the Butcher, Henry VI

Shakespeare's line about lawyers is often cited as a reference to the reckoning of corrupt practitioners of the law, but in fact it is the opposite. The world's most famous playwright meant it as a compliment, The notion of killing all the lawyers, the keepers of the law, was floated by Dick the Butcher as a means of causing civil unrest so the rebel Jack Cade could take control of the kingdom. The strategy is crude, but often effective, especially among those authoritarian types that see supreme power as a divine right; the kind of people that currently pay for Jordan Saint-Ives' expertise. Of course these are men whose success, despite being accidental, inherited, or stolen, has given them the mistaken impression that they are always the smartest people in the room; so they hire the best minds they can find and then proceed to ignore everything they advise. It is, therefore, no surprise that Saint-Ives' employers totally ignore his warnings and demand he plays Dick the Butcher to their Jack Cade. A *memorandum mortis* is issued for the ex ambulance chaser Artie Pearl.

The Hollywood and Highland Center is four floors of luxury shops, restaurants, theatres, and movie kitsch. Mo Fields sits under an umbrella on the second floor patio of the Crepe Café enjoying an overpriced coffee. He waits for his daughter Betty who has returned from school back East. He's promised to spend the afternoon treating her to a well-earned shopping spree and an expensive dinner. He scans the courtyard and spots her coming through the entrance of the bizarre Chinese theatre arches, a hodgepodge of misplaced symbols that combine vaguely reminiscent Egyptian reliefs with statues of welcoming elephants that have a similarly loose resemblance to something Hindu; cultural correctness was obviously not a high priority for the architects and designers.

Mo has arranged that Betty meet him at the café. As he waits for Betty to make her way up to the restaurant, he surveys the general area, a professional habit. Across the expanse of the courtyard on the other side of the mall he sees his old pal Artie Pearl. It reminded him that Artie is supposed to come into the shop to pick up his new suits. He watches as Artie goes into a boutique.

Someone is following him: female, thirty, blonde, nice legs and a pretty face, but hard. She's wearing gray designer slacks and a black leather jacket. She's someone that's earned her expensive outfit the hard way, and it shows. She's a professional, that's obvious: she keeps her distance while using display mirrors and reflective storefront glass to maintain visual contact.

As Artie comes out of the shop a gust of wind swirls through the open air balcony. It catches the woman's black leather jacket flipping it open revealing a nice body and a shoulder holster with what looks like a Glock, but it's hard to tell from so far away. Mo reaches inside his jacket but he's not carrying. No point bringing a gun to a shopping expedition for Betty, go figure.

Betty sits down at the table beside her father. She leans over and kisses him on the cheek. "Hi Dad. I hope you brought your wallet." Mo doesn't immediately answer. Betty follows her father's gaze. "She's pretty." Mo turns to his daughter and returns the kiss, "Hi dear."

Betty knows her father. She knows making suits isn't the only business her Dad is in. She doesn't know the details, and she doesn't want to know, but she knows Uncle Benson is someone important, someone who orders more than suits when he comes to the shop. She's seen his picture in the newspaper and read all the rumors about how he heads a major Chinese criminal organization, but as far as she's concerned he's just a nice old man who she's known her whole life.

Betty: "You working?"

Mo: "I don't know, something is off."

Betty: "That woman?"

Mo: "Remember my friend, Artie Pearl?"

Betty: "Sure, he's cute."

Mo: "It looks like that woman is following him."

Betty looks across the courtyard and sees the woman stop every time Artie stops to look in a window. "She's carrying a gun, maybe she's a cop?" Mo is surprised at his daughter's observation. "Don't be so surprised, I am your daughter. You think I don't know things?"

Mo: "You stay here and order some lunch. I'm going to say hello to Artie."

Betty: "I guess that big shopping spree is off?"

Mo: "I'll be right back. We'll have lots of time to go shopping." He gets up and heads out of the café. As he does, he takes out his cell phone and dials Artie's number. Artie's phone goes to his answering service, *"You've reached Arthur Pearl, I'm not available at this time, Please leave a message and I'll get back to you as soon as possible."* Mo leaves a message, *"Artie, it's Mo. You got a problem. You're being tailed."*

Betty watches as her father leaves the café. A waiter comes over to ask what she wants to order. Betty ignores him preoccupied with concern for her father. She watches as an older man with salt and pepper hair gets up and follows her father out of the restaurant. As he does, she sees he swipes a steak knife from a recently vacated table waiting to be cleared. The guy looks like one of the town's minor directors; you can't turn around in Hollywood without banging into someone in the movie business, but directors, even minor ones, don't steal steak knifes, besides everyone in Hollywood looks like an actor or director, even if they just sell shoes.

Waiter: "Miss... would you like to order?"

Betty: "Sorry... I have to leave." Betty gets up and follows the well-dressed director-type who is obviously tailing her father. She keeps well back trying to use the example of the pretty woman following her Dad's pal, Artie Pearl. As she watches the man's reflection in the window she notices a display of cheap wireless electric drills. She enters the store and goes directly to the display of drills. She picks up a box containing one of the drills. She takes it to the counter.

Betty: "Show me how this works?" The salesman starts into a long-winded sales pitch. "I don't care about that! Is the battery charged?"

Salesman: "The factory usually gives them a minor charge just to show people that it works, but you'll have to charge it properly for a couple of hours at least."

Betty: "Put the battery in for me."

Salesman: "I told you young lady, it's not really charged..."

Betty fumbles in her purse for her wallet. She pulls out twenty-five bucks and throws it on the counter. "You want to make the sale, put the damn battery in the drill. Now!" The salesman mumbles something about rude customers but does what he's told. He puts the battery in and hands it to Betty. She presses the trigger, and the drill comes to life.

The salesman gathers up the money on the counter, "I'll get your change." He turns and leaves for the cash register. Betty grabs the longest drill bit in the box and puts it in the drill. The salesman returns with Betty's change but she's not there. She left the store with the drill but the box, the extra drill bits, and the recharger are still sitting on the counter. He shakes his head.

The pretty assassin is closing in on Artie with Mo only a few yards behind. Artie makes a quick left turn into the isle labelled "Restrooms." The isle is empty. Mo closes quickly. The woman reaches under her black leather jacket just as she passes the entrance to the ladies room. The woman feels Mo's presence and turns quickly just in time to see Mo's fist come out of nowhere. Everything goes black.

The pretty assassin opens her eyes, She can already feel the swelling in her face. She focuses. Standing over her in the enclosed space of a bathroom stall is Mo Fields holding her gun. "Nice piece. I got one just like it." She rubs her reddened cheek where Mo hit her. "You hit me pretty hard. It hurts."

Mo: "Sorry about that, but I can't have you killing my friend. Under normal circumstances you'd be dead, but seeing I'm technically off duty, I'm prepared to make allowances. So from one professional to another, get the fuck out of town, your work here is done."

The woman gives Mo the once over. Maybe a swift kick in the nuts would even the score and give her the advantage. The bathroom stall is cramped, it wouldn't take much.

Mo: "I know what you thinking. Don't! You're far too attractive for me to mess up any more than I already have."

The woman smiles, "I heard about you. You're the tailor. I thought that was just a story."

Mo: "Do we have a deal or not?"

Woman: "I don't have much choice do I?"

Mo shrugs, "You could try, but it won't end well for you."

Woman: "Maybe we should part as friends."

Mo: "Okay then, you can sit and enjoy the ambience for ten minutes or I can hit you again to make sure you hang around for a while. What would you prefer?"

Woman: "I think I'll just stay put, my face doesn't need any more lumps."

Mo: "Good decision… I'll keep the gun." Mo opens the stall door just as a middle aged woman enters the bathroom. The woman sees Mo, "You can't be in here. This is the Ladies' Room."

Mo: "Get with it lady, You never heard of LGBT." The sound of pained laughter comes out of the stall behind Mo. The woman storms out of the restroom.

Artie exits the Men's Room. Jordan Saint-Ives is waiting Betty turns the corner into the isle labelled "Restrooms".

She holding the drill close to her side. Artie smiles when
he sees Betty. Saint-Ives readies the steak knife for a
quick lunge but as he does Betty nails him with the
electric drill. He drops the knife as he stifles a scream.
Mo comes out of the ladies' room carrying the gun. Saint-
Ives is doubled over in pain. He tries to straighten up but
Mo hits him across the face with the gun. Saint-Ives goes
down like he was hit by Mike Tyson in his prime.

Betty looks at her father, "Can we go shopping now?"

11
NEWTON'S THIRD LAW
**"For every action,
there is an equal and opposite reaction."**

Jordan Saint-Ives warned Management that there would be consequences if they tried to take out Artie Pearl. Despite her looks, Rita Daveed, AKA Rati Devi, is one hard *Jodekager*, the evidence of which is legendary in the secretive world of Israeli Intelligence. The boys in Glilot Junction noted more than once, "fuck with Rita, and she'll serve you your dick on a platter." If Sir Isaac would have known Rita, he may have adjusted his Third Law, noting that sometimes an action can cause an opposite and unequal reaction with unintended consequences of far greater impact than the original. If you want a fight, Rita Daveed would counter with a war.

When Rati heard about the incident at the Hollywood and Highland mall she was furious, but she remained calm. She calls Mo Fields to thank him for his help and Mo suggests she might want to contact certain people he knows that might be willing to help for a price. Rati agrees; so Mo Fields calls Benson Yeung, Dragon Head of the Hong Mian triad; Yeung calls Johnny Luck his chef lieutenant; and Luck calls his protégé, the pretty blonde Jesse James. Jesse speaks to her husband, financier and owner of Murphy Peanut Butter Corporation, William Stone. Stone's peanut butter operation is one of the largest cocaine distributors in the United States. The idea of expanding into the marijuana market is a logical business decision; the Hong Mian already distributes cocaine and ecstasy, so why not marijuana? It seems to be the ideal product for an organization whose expertise is blending legal and illegal components into a viable cohesive money-making strategy.

Despite the Federal governments unwillingness to accept the inevitable, marijuana is becoming increasingly more socially acceptable as multiple States rush to legalize the source of a potential tax revenue windfall. With Stone's financial and operational backing and Hong Mian's muscle, the Baba Bhang brand could be industrialized with state-of-the-art production and nationwide distribution in both legal and underground markets. But before any of that can happen, the Siniestro business has to be resolved, enter Genghis Lee, AKA The Khan.

Genghis Lee is head of distribution for Murphy Peanut Butter's less-than-legal product line. Although Lee now resembles a successful executive, his prior business experience involved running the Lion Dogs Motorcycle Gang, a street level distributor of cocaine for the Hong Mian. When the gang transitioned into the Murphy distribution department, Lee became Senior Logistics Manager. He combined the street-hard toughness of a gang leader with the savvy sophistication of a hard-nosed business executive, making him the ideal man to send to Siniestro to supervise the takeover of the county.

An enterprise of the magnitude envisioned by William Stone and his associates required local co-operation if not outright complicity, but that meant eliminating any stubborn obstacles like Mayor Malcolm C. Barnes and his oil hungry backers. Lee arrives and takes up residence in a suite at the Hindquarter Inn. The quaint California wine country community of Siniestro is about to become ground zero for a confrontation pitting the interests of psychotropic induced pleasure against the producers of petroleum-based pollution.

12
THE SINIESTRO COUNTY FEUD

The failed assault on Artie Pearl was meant to be a warning, but instead it turned out to be a declaration of war. Saint-Ives is blamed for the failure despite his advice against the attack. Management is intent on escalating the situation while Saint-Ives, knowing Rati Devi is merely the superficial alter ego of the far more dangerous and resourceful Rita Daveed, suggests negotiation, compromise, and if needed, a sharing of the potential wealth.

Management rejects the diplomatic approach out-of-hand; sharing just isn't in their DNA. A team of heavy duty muscle is sent to Siniestro to guarantee Rati and Baba Bhang get the message loud and clear: "sell or else." Twenty ex-military oil company mercenaries with experience in projecting their employers' influence throughout the world arrive in town. They set up headquarters at the Jepsen Hotel. The group is led by a stiff-backed, jarhead, Captain, Alfred McQuad, USMC, Retired.

It's two o'clock in the morning, Artie and Rati are in bed in Artie's room. They wake with a start. Their cell phones vibrate in unison on the bedside tables. Something must be wrong. They reach for their phones, it's the ex Shin Bet agents. The messages from each are exactly the same. "Get to the Center immediately, there's trouble." Artie calls Genghis Lee's room and tells him there's a problem and they all have to get to the Center now. Artie and Rati dress quickly. They take the stairs to the lobby not wanting to wait for the elevator. Genghis meets them in the lobby as he gets off the elevator. "What's going on?"

Artie: "We don't know, but it sounds bad."

Rati: "Call for reinforcements."

Genghis pulls out his phone as they run towards Rati's limo. The driver is already waiting with the car running. Rati called him when Artie called Genghis. They pile into the car and head out towards the Center. Genghis dials Stone's number. "William, it's Genghis. Send in the cavalry."

Ten minutes later they approach the gate to the Center, they can see the flames rising into the wine country night; tent city is ablaze. The staff including Baba and his three mistresses are doing what they can to help contain the fire. The flames don't reach the main building or winery, but tent city is completely gutted. Luckily there is only a handful of lingering disciples staying on the grounds as the last lecture series ended earlier in the week. No one is harmed, but tent city is completely destroyed. The Siniestro volunteer fire department arrives too late to do anything but put out the remaining embers making sure the flames don't restart near the winery or main building. The following day Saint-Ives and the rest of Siniestro is awakened by the sound of twenty-five Harley-Davidson motorcycles ridden by black-leather clad men wearing Lion Dog colors roaring down the center of Copenhagen Boulevard on their way to the Hindquarter Inn. Saint-Ives hears the noise and looks out his window. He watches the Lion Dogs pass. There's a knock on his room door. He opens it. It's McQuad, "You see what's going on out there?"

Saint-Ives: "I told you she wouldn't be intimidated."

McQuad: "We'll see. I doubt the lawyer and the old Indian have her willingness to fight."

Saint-Ives; "We should negotiate."

McQuad: "We don't get paid to talk."

Saint-Ives: "Well then, I hope you get paid enough to die."

13
RAGNAR'S DINER

Ragnar's Diner is a tourist trap aimed at attracting kids intent on a Nordic experience with their bacon and eggs. The owner, Ralf Simmons, AKA Ragnar, prowls the premises handing out Ragnar souvenir coloring books to underage Vikings, while appropriately dressed Shield Maidens serve the guests pancakes, waffles, and omelettes. The diner is located halfway between the Jepsen Hotel, headquarters for the forces of slimy black crude, and the Hindquarter Inn, where the alliance of psychedelic spiritual awakening has gathered. For the time being Ragnar's Diner is the Siniestro DMZ. Whatever tables aren't occupied by tourists, are filled with either tattooed Chinese Lion Dog gang members or mercenaries dressed in their battle fatigues. The children are impressed; their parents, not so much.

Saint-Ives and Captain McQuad sit at one end of the diner enjoying their ham and cheese omelettes, toast, and coffee, while Rati, Artie, and Genghis sample the French toast, maple syrup, and strawberries.

Saint-Ives gets up holding a white paper napkin above his head. He makes his way to where Rati, Artie, and Genghis Lee are sitting. "I come in peace."

Rati: "Put the napkin down Avrum, you look like an idiot."

Genghis looks at Artie, "If I shoot this motherfucker dead, can you get me off because he disturbed my breakfast?"

Artie mulls over the question: "The French toast disturbance defence, I'd have to check the Findlaw database, but I'm sure we'd set a precedent."

Rati points to the empty seat beside Genghis. Saint-Ives sits, "I had nothing to do with that fire. I told Management they should negotiate, make peace, there's enough damn money to make everyone happy, but these assholes aren't the sharing types."

Rati: "You want a fight, Avrum, you got one. You bring in soldiers; we bring an army. You start a fire; we blow up a building. You take out one of ours; we eliminate your entire Board of Directors. You fucked with the wrong people."

Saint-Ives sits quietly listening as Rati calmly describes her visceral reaction to the burning of tent city and the attempted murder of Artie Pearl. "Don't do it Rita, these people mean business. They don't understand who they're dealing with. Let me try to reason with them."

Rati: "Your people need to learn a lesson. Doesn't matter what your toy soldiers try, your employers will pay, maybe not today, maybe not tomorrow, maybe not for a year, but pay they will. My new partners have a long arm and an even longer memory. You're just lucky we have history or you'd be the first to go down."

Saint-Ives: "Let me speak to them, maybe they'll come to their senses. This whole thing has got out of hand. Reason has to prevail."

Rati: "You know better than that Avrum, you can't reason with religious fanatics."

Saint-Ives: "Aren't you describing your own band of crackpots? This whole Baba Bhang thing is nothing more than a cult."

Rati: "The only thing Baba preaches is a good time. His followers don't believe in anything more than good dope, a good meal, and a great lay. They're harmless fools. It's your employers that are the dangerous fanatics; they pray at the alter of petro dollars. So you tell me, Avrum, who's the crackpot? Which one is the real cult?"

Saint-Ives: "Give me a couple days to reason with them."

Rati: "You've got till four o'clock today."

Saint-Ives gets up to leave, "Four o'clock then; I'll get back to you. I'm trying to avoid violence Rita. I'm not looking for a war. You know I was at the mall to make sure it didn't go too far. My arm still hurts from whatever your people stuck in me."

Rati: "Mess with a snake and you're liable to get bit."

Saint-Ives: "Understood. I'll get back to you before four." He leaves the diner.

Genghis looks at Rati, "So you want me to hold off?"

Artie interrupts, "Fuck'em, call Mo, These assholes need to know we're serious." Rati looks at Genghis "Do it. We need to know your people are prepared to go all in."

14
MANAGEMENT REVEALED
**"Merchants have no country. The mere spot they stand on does not constitute so strong an attachment as that from which they draw their gains."
– Thomas Jefferson, 1814**

Texas Tom Torkild is a Theodore Roosevelt look-alike complete with pince-nez wire-frame glasses and a Wilshire Boulevard office filled with the heads of dead endangered species on his walls; trophies he won in a poker game rather than facing the wild beasts, *mano a mano*. Torkild is just that sort of man, the kind that employs others to do his dirty work; the kind of business executive, Thomas Jefferson referred to when he uttered the Capitalist-crushing sentiment, "merchants have no country." American business has an unfortunate history of collaborating with the enemy, a fact few like to talk about. As far as Texas Tom Torkild is concerned, what's good for Torkild Energy Corporation is good for the USA, and that goes for the wine stain on the map known as Siniestro, California.

Texas Tom Torkild is neither Texan nor Danish as the name implies. The colorful Texas moniker was self-anointed after sitting on the bench as a third string linebacker for the Texas Longhorns when they beat the Fighting Irish in a long-forgotten Cotton Bowl. He's a self-made man whose nickname is not the only aspect of his carefully crafted image that was invented rather than earned or inherited.

Torkild found his way to fame and fortune through sheer dumb luck. As a young conman, he borrowed enough of a stake to purchase a New Mexico farm in the Permian Basin that he used to raise roosters for cock-fighting. He hoped to make it big by supplying killer-chickens to

Mexican aficionados of the disgusting excuse for a sport. The cock-fighting plan fell apart because Torkild knew nothing about raising chickens. Before he had a chance to sell the farm he was approached by some oilmen who wanted to buy his property. Instead of selling he cleverly made a deal making him a partner in the operation.

Once he was in, it was only a matter of time before he squeezed out his partners. What Torkild didn't know about oil was overcome by hiring experts. He grew the company using tried-and-true business practices like political payoffs and shady land deals. Torkild's publicity department promoted his rags-to-riches rise as the embodiment of the American dream; a far kinder interpretation of the facts that in reality came closer to Lucky Luciano's climb from obscurity than to a Horatio Alger novel.

Torkild sits at the end of what feels like a twenty-foot long solid walnut boardroom table. Saint-Ives occupies the high-backed leather chair at the opposite end of the table facing his boss. Outside this room Torkild is only referred to as Management. Mayor Barnes recovered from his overindulgence in Baba's liquid samples sits on one side of Saint-Ives while on the other side, still looking a little green at the gills, is Sheriff Tomkins. Saint-Ives starts to say something, but Torkild raises his hand signalling silence. Torkild presses a button on the intercom. The head of security for Torkild Energy enters and walks to where Saint-Ives is sitting. He sticks out his hand.

Security Man: "Your phone."

Torkild looks at Saint-Ives "Give him your phone." He turns to Mayor Barnes and the Sheriff. "You two as well. There are no phones allowed in this room. You'll get them back when you leave."

Torkild looks at Saint-Ives: "What seems to be the problem? This should be a simple matter. The fire must have made them rethink their position. Throw some money at the Indian and be done with it. If I knew you couldn't handle some third world beauty queen and her ambulance chaser boyfriend, I never would have sent you in the first place."

Saint-Ives: "I told you that wouldn't work. The guru is irrelevant. Your so-called beauty queen is ex IDF and Shin Bet and her ambulance chaser boyfriend turns out to be smarter than we thought."

Torkild: "So what? They're two people, we're a multi-billion-dollar corporation. You told me that woman would scare them off, but the two of you ended up looking like you went ten rounds with Ali. Now you've got a small army sitting in that gingerbread shit-hole." Torkild looks at Mayor Barnes and the Sheriff, "No offense." He focuses his glare back on Saint-Ives, "You've got the men, use them."

Saint-Ives: "You're being ridiculous. They've got a Chinese triad motorcycle gang sitting at the other end of town. You want a goddamn Tong War in the middle of town?"

Sheriff Tomkins: "We can't have Copenhagen Boulevard turned into a war zone."

Mayor Barnes: "It will kill tourism."

Torkild: "Enough with all the whining, so things get a little rough. You two clowns will have lots of dough to rebuild things after we take over. That whole Danish thing is stupid, anyway."

Mayor Barnes: "Aren't you Danish? I mean Torkild that's Danish."

Torkild laughs: "Don't be daft. I'm Italian. My grandfather's name was Torigini. He couldn't get work as an Italian so he changed it. He thought people would prefer Danes. Schmuck... this is America, we don't like anybody."

Saint-Ives: "Maybe we can let them stay and we'll just purchase the oil rights. That way everyone is happy. I don't understand why we didn't take that approach in the first place."

Torkild: "Forget it. A little crude drips on their precious grapes and they'll be all up in arms. They need to go. Let McQuad deal with them. If they thought burning a few tents was the limit to our ability, they better think again."

Saint-Ives: "You're making a mistake. I'm out. You don't know who you're dealing with. People are going to get killed."

Torkild: "Fine! You're out. You're useless anyway."

Saint-Ives gets up and leaves. He retrieves his cell phone from security and heads for the elevator. The Mayor and the Sheriff remain for some additional brow-beating. As Saint-Ives rides down the elevator from the executive offices of the Torkild Energy Building, he dials Rati, "Rita, it's Avrum. Think you can find me a room at the Hindquarter, it's time to get on the right side of this mess."

15
DINNER IS A BLAST

Rati, Artie, and Genghis Lee enter Carnivore's Cavern, a neutral Beverly Hills eatery acceptable to both sides. The place is favored by those Hollywood types that prefer bloody slabs of steak or roast beef rather than raw fish wrapped in sticky rice; better to have bloody sirloin on your plate than blood splatter on your walls, not that Genghis couldn't be convinced to have his men redecorate the place with Texas Tom's gray matter.

Sitting waiting in the far corner is Texas Tom Torkild himself, along with Mayor Barnes and Sheriff Tomkins. Enjoying a thick, juicy steak in the middle of the dinning room with a clear view of Torkild's table is Mo Fields. Facing him with his back to Torkild is Field's dinning partner, Jordan Saint-Ives. Several of Genghis Lee's Lion Dog associates are sprinkled around the restaurant, their elaborate tattoos and gangland personas nicely disguised by custom suits supplied by Mo Fields. Although no physical violence is anticipated, Lee is taking no chances. He insists his new charges be adequately protected.

Torkild looks at the threesome sitting opposite, "So, who am I talking to, the Indian drug pusher, the shyster Jew, or the Chinaman?" Rati doesn't react. The hair on the back of Artie's neck stands up, but he says nothing. Lee just smiles. He's heard all the ethnic slurs before, it will take more than a few adolescent insults to get him to react, besides, vengeance is best delivered unexpectedly, perhaps while enjoying a shave and a haircut like Albert Anastasia, or maybe while riding one of his paid female friends like something out of a Tarantino movie while *You Know I'm No Good* by Amy Winehouse plays on the stereo.

Rati: "You called this meeting, what do you want?"

Torkild looks at Rati, "Okay… it's the Maharishi's bitch. No wonder things are so fucked up. I have to give you credit though. These clowns would have caved long ago. You got balls, lady, I'll give you that, but you don't have Israeli Intelligence in your back-pocket anymore, and a Jew lawyer and some Chinese muscle just won't cut it. You're dealing with oil business now Honey, and when it comes to crude, what's good for Torkild Energy is good for America. You see. I've got the whole goddamn US government in my back-pocket. I'm a fucking patriot."

Rati: "Other than insults and threats, you got anything else to offer?"

Torkild: "Sure, I'm a generous guy, I could just take what I want but I'm feeling magnanimous. I'll give you three million for the property. Take it or leave it."

Rati: "Your former representative made a much more generous offer."

Torkild: "And that's why he's a former employee."

Rati does not take her eyes off of Torkild, "What do you think Artie, my love, should we take Mr. Torkild's offer?"

Artie: "Now why would we do that when Magen Industries is offering us fifty million just for the oil rights, plus a percentage of the revenue produced, and we retain ownership of the land." Artie shifts his gaze to Mayor Barnes, "In fact our representative, Tyler Raines, is in Yafo now, discussing details."

Mayor Barnes: "Goddamn it! I kill that son-of-a-bitch."

Torkild doesn't answer immediately, absorbing the news that he has a competitor, an Israeli conglomerate and military contractor with strong ties to both the Israeli and US governments. "You've been a busy boy Mr. Pearl. Saint-Ives said we underestimated you, but it *ain't* going to happen. One phone call and your alternative bid will die, and if it doesn't, perhaps then one of you."

Sheriff Tomkin: "Now just a minute, Tom, I'm the goddamn Sheriff. You can't be threatening people. We need to do this legally."

Torkild: "Sure, sure, don't get your knickers in a twist. It's just a colourful turn of phrase."

Genghis turns to Artie and Rati, "It doesn't look like these assholes are even going to buy us dinner. How about we go for some Chinese food, I know a place?" They get up and leave for a more hospitable dinning experience.

Torkild and company order dinner and discuss their next move. The Lion Dog associates all finish their dinners and leave. Fields and Saint-Ives linger over coffee and dessert waiting for Torkild to leave. When they do Fields and Saint-Ives split up, with Saint-Ives heading back to Siniestro while Fields follows Torkild.

Saint-Ives takes the short walk to his Aston Martin enjoying the LA night air. He climbs into the sports car and his cell phone rings. It's Torkild. Saint-Ives mutters, "What the hell does he want?" He hesitates, should he answer or should he let it ring? "Fuck it." He answers on the third ring. BOOM!

Standing between two buildings about half a block away is the Head of Torkild Security, the same guy that took Saint-Ives' cell phone in the Torkild boardroom. He walks over to the curb. He dismantles the prepaid phone and drops the pieces in the sewer. As he starts walking away in the opposite direction, he can hear the sound of fire engines responding to the explosion.

65

16
FOR EVERY ACTION

The appearance of the Lion Dogs in Siniestro was intended only as a show of force to counter McQuad's mercenaries and to signal no more attacks would be tolerated. On the ground, the situation was a standoff with Genghis Lee's Lion Dogs at one end of town and McQuad's outfit at the other.

The attempted assassination of Artie and the burning of tent city were each provocation enough, but the successful murder of Saint-Ives demanded a response. If Torkild figured Rati would let the Saint-Ives killing slide, he was mistaken. His miscalculations were beginning to add up: first, he misread Saint-Ives' personal connection to Rati Devi; second, he underestimated Artie Pearl's ability to find a competitive bid; third, he never connected the dots that linked Artie to Fields and Fields to the Chinese; and lastly, he miscalculated Rati's visceral reaction to the death of her friend and intelligence colleague.

There are many ways to kill: shooting stabbing, poisoning, accidents, and artificially induced heart attacks, but a bombing is more that just a murder, it's a message, and the message was heard loud and clear. The Lion Dogs relocated to the hastily reconstructed tent city on the grounds of the Baba Bhang complex. The Center was now an armed camp, protected and patrolled by leather clad Chinese gang members.

Rati, Artie, and Genghis Lee all gather in the Baba Bhang boardroom. Rati turns to Artie, "Any word from Tyler."

Artie: "They're putting the deal together now. I've set up a new corporation, Avrum Industries…"

Rati: "That's very sweet my love, thank you."

Artie: "The company is a fifty-fifty partnership between BBE and Murphy Peanut Butter as agreed to by you and Stone. You'll both have to go to Yafo to sign the papers when Tyler tells me they're ready. Most of the financial details have been agreed to in principle, but they're concerned we don't have the muscle to protect their investment."

Rati: "We have to respond, but we got to be smart about how we do it. Avrum was a friend and his death has to be revenged, and not just as a sign to Magen that we can handle our end of the deal."

Genghis: "You leave that to me. I spoke with Stone this morning and he approved my purchase of a new suit, actually a whole wardrobe. I'm going to LA this afternoon to speak to the tailor to pick out just the right fabric."

Late that afternoon Genghis Lee enters the Three Kings Tailor Shop in Beverly Hills. The shop is busy. William Stone is in the middle of a try-on with Fields' head tailor marking the sleeve of an unfinished suit jacket while Jesse James, Stone's wife, advises Johnny Luck on which fabric to buy. The discussion soon shifts from haberdashery to revenge.

17
SHALOM

Artie, Rati, William Stone, and Joseph, one of her two Shin Bet security guards, land at Ben Gurion Airport around eight-thirty in the morning Israeli time. They are met by Tyler Raines who has been working with the Magen lawyers to iron-out the details of the contract. Raines has been in close contact with Artie who has been monitoring his progress. Genghis Lee and Rati's other security man have stayed in Siniestro to keep an eye on Baba to make sure McQuad doesn't try to take him out in their absence, figuring without the goofy guru, Rati's whole business plan falls apart.

The short nineteen kilometre drive from the airport to Yafo doesn't take long. Yafo, or Jaffa if you prefer, is the oldest part of Tel Aviv with shops, restaurants, and ancient alleys crammed with hidden historic and tourist treasures at every turn. It's a beautiful day, and the weather is delightful but warm. The streets of Yafo are crowded with tourists scouting for souvenirs and locals scurrying about trying to get their shopping done before the midday heat starts to take effect. Raines babbles on about the contract as he manoeuvres his way through the streets to their ultimate location, the historic Suskin House, where the Magen lawyers have their offices. Raines has worked hard to impress Artie; he's enjoyed every bit of his newfound responsibilities enhanced by the intrigue of an exciting international adventure.

The Suskin House is hidden behind a series of ancient stone buildings that border a series of narrow twisted alleys that wind their way in a maze-like fashion to the historic building that overlooks the harbour where Jonah famously set sail for his encounter with the whale. Rati,

Artie, and Stone are in the backseat, with Joseph, the ex Shin Bet agent, up front with Raines.

Rati: "Did you get the tools?"

Raines: "It's under the passenger seat." Joseph reaches under the seat and pulls out a Glock 26 Sub-Compact Semi Automatic, Rati's firearm of choice.

Joseph: "You were supposed to get two."

Raines: "That's all they gave me."

Joseph hands it to Rati, but she shakes her head. "You hold on to it. I doubt any of our old enemies know we're here, anyway." Joseph places the gun beside him on the seat.

Tyler turns his head to face the passengers in the back, "We're going to have to park around here and walk. The Suskin House is at the end of the alley."

Just as Raines turns his head back, he spots an Arab woman pushing a baby carriage across the street right in front of the car. He slams on the brakes just barely avoiding hitting the baby carriage. The force of the sudden stop knocks the Glock onto the floor of the car.

The woman reaches into the carriage as if to console her child, but instead she pulls out a Kalashnikov assault rifle and starts yelling something in Arabic. The screams are muffled by the car, but Rati clearly makes out the name of her old, Prince Fahed.

The woman tries to fire the weapon but it jams. Joseph jumps out of the car and runs toward the woman just as she gets the rifle to fire. She hits him in the chest with a burst from the weapon. Joseph stumbles forward landing on the woman knocking the AK-47 onto the road. Rati throws open the backdoor of the car and grabs Artie by the collar flinging herself and him out of the car and onto the stone sidewalk. Stone jumps out of the other side of the car and heads for the rifle. The woman looks at the rifle and then Stone, she decides to run. She takes off down the alley towards the harbor. Stone picks up the rifle and goes after her.

The alley is a convoluted labyrinth of serpentine twists and turns and side alleys leading to more alleys and dead ends. Stone runs down the alley until he come to a small round-about where the alley splits off into multiple directions like the spokes of a wheel. He stops not knowing which direction to try. An old man opens a blue painted iron gate, steps out onto the street, and whistles, attracting Stone's attention. Stone wheels quickly raising the Russian-made killing machine in the direction of the old man. The old man raises his arm pointing down one of the spokes of the stone wheel. Stones nods and takes off down the alley. He runs down the alley where it makes an abrupt turn only to find it's a dead end. He hears the creaking sound of one of the iron gates that front the entrances to the buildings. He turns readying the AK to fire. The Arab woman steps out into the street from behind the gate. She holding a pistol, but Stone is too quick. He fires as walks straight toward her and he keeps on firing. The woman's body is flung backwards into the gate as it contorts sporadically from the continuous burst from the rifle. The woman is cut to shreds. William Stone, ex British military, ex British intelligence, ex a lot of things is the wrong guy to point a weapon at.

The rest of the day is spent answering questions from the local police, Israeli Shin Bet, and numerous other officials. A lawyer from Magen Industries arrives at the police station to see if everyone is alright. He informs

Rati and Artie that the Americans put pressure on the cabinet to kill the deal. Texas Tom Torkild played his ultimate ace, political influence. The deal with Magen Industries is dead, and unfortunately so is Rati's friend and colleague, Joseph.

The Baba Bhang operation had lost its focus. The oil deal was always a wild card, it was never part of the original plan that centered on cannabis, not oil. Artie convinces Rati that it's time to get back to basics. They discuss their decision with Stone who agrees. The oil isn't going anywhere; now is the time to focus on building the Baba Bhang brand with the winery and distillery providing the signature product offerings. In order to do that, they had to find a way to get Torkild off their backs. The Israeli trip was a disaster, but at least it provided clarity, unfortunately at the price of a young man's life.

Back in Siniestro, things weren't going much better. When Rati and company arrive back in California they are greeted at the airport by Genghis Lee who informs them that Baba and his three mistresses have been picked up by U.S. Immigration and Custom Enforcement agents and are being held awaiting a deportation hearing. If Baba is deported everything falls apart.

18
ONE MAN'S LIFESTYLE IS ANOTHER MAN'S…

Artie and Raines go to court to have the deportation orders cancelled. Artie argues that Baba is in the country legally, he has a valid visa, and he has not broken any laws. Artie shows evidence that Baba is a spiritual leader for thousands of US citizens that follow his teachings, and he is a peaceful, productive member of Siniestro County. He argues the three females also have valid visas and are employees of BBE LLC. The arrest and deportation of Baba Bhang and the three women is without merit and should be set aside.

The Assistant District Attorney argues Baba and the three women should be deported because Baba is a bigamist and the three women are his wives. The Judge asks the DA if he has any evidence that Baba is married to the three women, The only evidence the DA presents are driver's licenses showing that Baba and the three women all live at the same address. Artie explains, living at the same address is not evidence of bigamy, and in fact, the address is the headquarters for BBE LLC and the living quarters for Baba's personal staff.

Artie points out, California law considers bigamy a misdemeanor "wobbler" offense, and therefore, does not rise to the level of moral turpitude, and not a deportable offense. But since there is no real evidence that the three women are anything but employees of the company, the Judge has no option but to dismiss the charges and cancel the deportation.

The Judge listens carefully to both sides. When the arguments are finished, he turns to the DA and lambasts him for bringing such a trivial matter to court, wasting his valuable time and the taxpayers' money. He points out that he cannot but wonder if there are underlying influences and commercial pressures at play in the governments desire to deport four productive members of society. The deportation order is cancelled and Baba and the three woman are set free.

19
HOLI RESOLUTION

With Magen Industries backing out of the BBE deal, Torkild feels he is home free. The effort to deport Baba Bhang and his women didn't work, but Torkild believes the show of political influence and reach has to be giving Rati Devi and her friends second thoughts. First, there was the attempt on Artie Pearl's life; it didn't work, but it showed just how far Torkild is prepared to go. Second, there was the intimidation by McQuad and company, and the burning of tent city. Third, was the murder of Rati's friend and former colleague, Jordan Saint-Ives. Fourth, was a show of political clout by forcing Magen Industries to kill their deal with BBE. Fifth, was the terrorist attack, perpetrated by Middle East oil partner Prince Fahed who was more than willing to get even with Rati for past encounters. And finally, the bigamy charge and threat of deportation intended to create a moral backlash against Baba Bhang and his free love lifestyle.

Torkild feels confident his tactics are working; and so as a man not inclined to waste money, he orders Captain McQuad to withdraw and report for his next assignment in the Middle East. Torkild figured it was only a matter of time before Rati and Artie Pearl come to the conclusion they must sell. It's the rational thing to do. Not bowing to the lord of oil's will is a mistake, a deadly mistake that already cost Jordan Saint-Ives and Joseph, the security agent, their lives. What Torkild didn't count on is Artie's willingness to stick by Rati, and Rati's determination to "fuck-up Torkild, real bad."

And so, that brings us to Holi.
The Hindu festival of Holi, the Festival of Color, is celebrated throughout the world by Hindus and non-Hindus alike. It is a celebration of Spring, of renewal, and

of the triumph of good over evil. It is a time where class distinction and cultural norms are forgotten, with everyone from high society and low, participating in the frantic joy of covering each other with colored powders, before drenching friends and strangers alike with water from special water guns called *pichkaris*. The spirit of fun and utter abandonment is enhanced by consuming copious amounts of Bhang Lassi.

The evening Holi begins is called Holika Dahan. A large ritual bonfire is created and people pray to rid themselves of evil by celebrating the burning of the evil demon Holika who was destroyed by fire. People rub the ashes from the fire onto their foreheads. According to legend the evil demon King Hiranyakashipu was pissed off at his son Prahlad who was a disciple of Vishnu.

Hiranyakashipu felt that he was the supreme god because he could not be killed by any conventional means. Hiranyakashipu felt Prahlad's following of Vishnu was disrespectful, so he ordered his sister, Holika, who wears a special flame resistant cloak to take Prahlad onto a burning pyre, but Vishnu creates a strong wind blowing open Holika's cloak so that it uncovers Holika and covers Prahlad. The evil Holika is consumed by the fire and Prahlad lives.

The following day is Rangwali Holi where people gather in the streets, toss colored powder all over one another and spray each with water in celebrating Krishna's love of Radha. When Krishna was a baby, the demon Putana tried to kill Krishna by poisoning him with her breast milk, but instead of killing him it only turned his skin blue. As Krishna grew into a man he fell in love with the beautiful and fair-skinned Radha.
Krishna was embarrassed by his dark blue skin. He complained to his mother, Yashoda, until she finally got fed up with his complaining and suggested he just throw

some colored powder on Radha solving the problem, and so the tradition of Holi was born.

Holika Dahan

The call went out across the States for Baba's followers to gather for a massive Holi celebration of food and fun, all fuelled by copious amounts of colored powder and free Bhang Lassi. Everyone is instructed to come in traditional Baba-like saffron attire and if they didn't have such an outfit, one would be provided for them as well as free *gulal*, the colored powders that make Holi the Festival of Color. Free *pichkari* water guns are also supplied to add some cooling relief from the midday California sun. As it happens, California is suffering an extraordinarily warm Spring with temperatures approaching, and sometimes surpassing, one hundred degrees Fahrenheit.

Hundreds of pleasure seekers arrive in Siniestro on the afternoon of Holika Dahan, some devoted followers of Baba Bhang and some just looking for free weed and a good time. The "Bhangers," the nickname given to them by the local media, are all transported to The Baba Bhang Center for a night of Holika Dahan debauchery. In the morning ten luxury coaches arrive to take the partygoers to the offices of Torkild Energy where the roughly one thousand Bhangers are instructed to let loose with a rainbow of *gulal* and fully loaded *pichkaris*. Among the saffron-clad celebrants are twenty Lion Dog gang members whose *gulal* and *pichkaris* are mixed with peroxide acetone a substance that is highly explosive when exposed to high temperatures, friction, static electricity, or shock.

Rangwali Holi

Los Angeles is being subjected to the warmest Spring on record. The midday temperatures in Hollywood where the Torkild Energy Building is located have reached triple digits. People are warned to hydrate and wear sunscreen. Workers are told to be careful when getting in their cars if they've been sitting outside all day. The Torklid Energy parking area is located outside and beside the Torklid building. You can literally fry a steak on the roof of everyone's car, including Torkild's luxury Mercedes Maybach S-Class.

The ten bus loads of Bhangers arrive in front of the Torklid Building, just about the time when Texas Tom Torkild heads for his Friday afternoon round of golf. The saffron revealers flood onto Wilshire Boulevard like a Tsunami of orange cotton. They quietly form two neat rows on the sidewalk, one on each side of the street.

A DJ and his crew unload a huge sound system and start to construct a makeshift stage in the center of Wilshire facing the Torkild Energy parking lot. Tourists, shoppers, and workers all start to gather wondering what is going on. The curious onlookers are greeted by Bhangers who hand them bags of yellow, green. orange, blue, and red *gulal* and loaded *pichkari* water guns. Lion Dog associates set up roadblocks at both the ends of the block. Another group of Lion Dogs dressed like Bhangers go to the Torklid parking lot to find Torkild's Mercedes. They cover it multi in colored *gulal* mixed with pure acetone peroxide. Pure acetone Peroxide gives off a fragment fruity smell.

A twenty-eight foot long white Lincoln limousine drives down the street and parks right in front of the Torkild building. The street is lined with saffron-clad Bhangers all standing at attention not moving, just waiting. The doors of the limo open and Baba Bhang and his three mistresses exit along with Rati Devi, Artie Pearl, Tyler Raines, and William Stone. They make their way to the stage in the middle of the street, and climb the wooden stairs provided and line up on either side of the DJ. Baba comes forward, his head swivelling like a helicopter with a damaged tail rotor blade. He has a big smile on his face. He raises his arms in the air signalling the Bhangers to form circles up and down Wilshire Boulevard. The DJ starts a rhythmic bass drum beat. The beat pounds hypnotically as the tourists, shoppers, and workers all wonder what is about to happen. Almost everyone in the Torkild building has come out of their offices and gone down to the street. As they leave the building Bhangers hand them bags of *gulal* and loaded *pichkaris*.

Torkild looks out his penthouse office window and curses, "What the fuck are those fools doing?" He turns to McQuad who has come to discuss his next assignment. "You better get me the hell out of here."

McQuad comes to the window and looks out. "You're safer where you are. Let's just wait and see what they have up their sleeve. We don't want to walk into a trap."

Down on the street platform, Baba smiles. His Don King silver, black, and gray hair glistens in the California sun. The pounding beat of the bass quickens. The crowd can feel the force of the rhythm in their chests.

Baba counts down, "Five, four, three, two, one…" *What Is Love* by Haddaway starts to blast out of the huge loud speakers… "*What is Love? Baby don't hurt me, Don't hurt me no more…*" The one thousand and twenty-eight Bhangers simultaneously toss their multi-colored gulal in the air creating an explosion of color.

The music fills the street *"What is Love? Baby don't hurt me, Don't hurt me no more..."* The Bhangers are all dancing and spraying each other with their *pichkaris.*

The music continues, and each time Haddaway sings *"What is Love?"* the Bhangers toss more *gulal* into the air. Everyone in the street is covered in colored powder including the bystanders who are not just watching but participating in the fun. One woman still holding her Coach purse and Gucci shopping bag is crowd surfing through the Bhangers being passed around like the Stars and Stripes at a major college bowl game. The music continues with everyone dancing, kissing, and drenching each other in water and *gulal* every time the *"What is Love?"* lyric is sung.

McQuad looks down upon the mayhem below, "I better get you out of here now before that mob tries to enter the building. We should take the stairs." McQuad and Torkild race down the stairs as quick as they can and exit the back entrance that leads to the parking lot. McQuad turns to Torkild, "Which one is your car?"

Torkild looks around not seeing his car. Then he realizes the one car in the parking lot covered in red, orange, blue, and green *gulal* is his. "Son-of-a-bitch!" He points to his car, "That one." They run towards the Mercedes. Torkild gets in the back and McQuad gets in the driver's seat. Both their hands are covered in *gulal.*

Torkild: "What is that smell?"

McQuad smells his hands covered in red and orange powder, "It's the powder... Jesus Christ, it's..." But before he can get the words out of his mouth, four saffron dressed Lion Dogs' throw firecrackers on the roof of the car and run like hell for cover.

The explosion is loud, with car and body parts flying in all directions. The crowd on the street just assumes the noise is part of the festivities.

The music continues... *"What is love? Baby don't hurt me. Don't hurt me no more..."* Rati turns to Artie and takes his hand, "My Love..." Artie kisses her.

EPILOGUE

Wall Street didn't take the news of Texas Tom Torkild's demise very well. He ran the company like it was his own private fiefdom never developing the infrastructure needed to sustain a major corporation. Without the domineering potentate of oil barking orders and issuing demands, the company stock went into free-fall, allowing a consortium of interests to take control at bargain basement prices.

Torkild Energy still had substantial oil interests and despite Torkild's authoritarian rule, the company was profitable. The consortium renamed the company HMM Energy, or if you prefer, Hancock, Murphy, Magen Energy. William Stone became Chairman of the Board, Artie Pearl was named CEO, and the newly divorced, Tyler Raines was announced as General Counsel. Benson Yeung, Johnny Luck, and Mrs. Rita Daveed Pearl were named to the Board of Directors; and Baba Bhang was named Director of Corporate Morale.

On the downside, no oil was ever found on the old Millbrook property, but with the laws restricting marijuana falling like dominos across the country, the sale of Baba's Bhang Lassi skyrocketed, followed by Bhang infused vodka and rum. There may not be oil in Siniestro but there is liquid gold.

Three Years Later

Men by nature are creatures of habit. Some say lazy, but creatures of habit sounds better. Normally, the consequences of ritual are benign, but sometimes habits, even innocuous ones like staying in the same hotel, can come back and bite you in the ass. And so, Prince Fahed arrived at the Claridge's Hotel as he always does when he visits London. As usual, the first thing he does after checking-in is contact the Head of Hotel Security, Lionel Norton, a man who earned his stripes working as a stringer for British intelligence. The Claridge's job was a nice retirement gig generating generous perks from wealthy guests for providing special services like the best call girls in town. A service frequently used by the Assistant Deputy of Finance in the Saudi Council of Ministers.

The Santi Joshi incident was only a faint memory for Fahed. It took some time, money, and a few dead bodies, but ultimately Fahed was able to cleanup his ill-advised Iranian investments, delete any traces of the evidence, and wipe the department computers of any and all invading viruses. The Israeli's no longer had his nuts in a vice. He was, as they say in the racing business, *home and cooled out.*

Fahed steps out of the shower and wraps himself in a large soft bath towel with the hotel's crest embroidered on it. The hotel phone on the bedside table rings. It's Lionel Norton, "Your highness, your guest has arrived, should I send her up?"

Fahed: "Is she what I ordered?"

Norton: "Yes Sir, very attractive… the best yet if you don't mind me saying so?"

Fahed: "Very good Lionel. If she is as good as advertised, I'll leave you a bonus in the morning."

Norton: "Very good Sir, most generous… Have an enjoyable evening."

Fahed: "Goodnight Lionel."

Norton: "Goodnight Sir." Lionel hangs up the phone in his office. Sitting opposite him is William Stone, a friend from the old days when both were active in British intelligence. The thing about the spy business is, once you're in, you're in for life, whether you're active or not. You just never know when an old chum will pop by and say, "Hello mate… I need someone dead."

Stone: "Does she know what to do?" Norton nods.

Fahed's Hotel Room Several Hours Later

The naked, dark-haired call girl slides out of Fahed's bed. On the way to the bathroom she grabs her small purse that contains her ID, her phone, and the twenty-five hundred dollars Fahed paid. She goes into the bathroom and closes the door. She takes her phone out of her purse and texts: 'I'm leaving now.' She flushes the toilet without using it. She runs the water as if to wash her hands. She goes back into the bedroom and retrieves her white silk blouse from the upholstered chair. She slips it on. She pulls her black, designer skirt over her hips and tucks in the blouse. She grabs her purse and starts to leave.

Fahed stirs, "Come back tonight, same time." The woman nods. She leaves the bedroom and makes her way through the suite. She gets to the door and hesitates. It's too late to turn back now; she's already sent the text. She opens the door.

A blonde hotel maid wearing plastic gloves is in the hall shuffling through various cleaning supplies on her cart. The maid hands the hooker an envelope. The hooker takes the envelope without looking at the maid and without stopping. She doesn't want to see her face; she doesn't want to know anything. She just wants to get to the parking garage as quickly as possible.

The maid wheels her cart into Fahed's room. She retrieves her Glock 26 Sub-Compact Semi Automatic with silencer from the lower tray of her cart. She enters the bedroom.

Fahed rolls over: "You're back for seconds?" He looks at the maid. "It's you!"

Rita aims at his chest. "For Joseph..." She pulls the trigger three times... POP! POP! POP! She walks over to the bed and puts another slug into his forehead. POP!

She takes her cart and wheels it out of the room to the cleaning station at the end of the hall. She removes the plastic gloves, her maid's outfit, and the blonde wig. She pulls an oversized purse out from the lower tray of the cart. She removes a black dress and heels from the bag. She dresses quickly. She shoves her disguise in the purse. She makes her way to the stairwell and down the stairs to the garage where a car is waiting. Artie is in the backseat with Mo Fields behind the wheel. William Stone comes out of the stairwell door a few minutes later. He gets in the car.

Fields: "The cameras?"

Stone: "Technical glitches, Lionel has been telling them for months they need to be replaced." They sit back and relax as Mo Fields maneuvers out of the parking garage and into London traffic. In an hour they'll be on a plane for New York and a few days of rest and relaxation.

Rita turns to Artie; she takes his hand, "My Love." Artie kisses her on the cheek.

THE END

BHANG LASSI
BACKGROUND AND RECIPE

There are three main gods in the Hindu religion, Shiva, Vishnu, and Brahman who are considered the creators of the universe. Shiva is the destroyer, the force responsible for renewal, and the god of cannabis. There are several cannabis creation stories. In one legend, in a time before creation of the universe, the gods decided to stir the great ocean of matter creating Amrita, the syrup of everlasting life. According to the tale, some potion dripped onto the earth and where it landed cannabis plants grew. Shiva was poisoned by *halahala* a substance produced during the creation of Amrita. In order to heal and sustain his life, Shiva consumed the cannabis plants that grew on earth where the Amrita fell. Shiva became a devoted cannabis user often represented in deep meditation with eyes half-shut smoking pot out of a chillum hookah. The drinking of Bhang Lassi honors Shiva, aids meditation, and cleanses your sins, or so it is believed.

The word Baba is an honorific meaning father and Bhang is cannabis, and so the fictional cult leader in our story, Baba Bhang, is literally the Father Pot.

Author's Note: While researching ideas for the book I ran a cross a recipe for Bhang Lassi that I thought might interest some people. I personally don't use pot and I don't drink, so I can't say this information is reliable, accurate, or even safe, but I thought it would be of general interest. If you search the Web, you can find numerous variations of Bhang drinks and eatables, including some that include alcohol. Over indulgence seems to be a risk, so as in all things, moderation should be considered.

Bhang Lassi
(timesofindia.com recipe)

Ingredients of Bhang Lassi
2 cups yoghurt (curd)
1/2 cup ice cubes
1/2 cup sugar
2 drops rose essence
1/2 cup sour cream
1 cup water
1/2 teaspoon bhang seed powder

Recipe for Bhang Lassi
Step 1: In a bowl, add yoghurt, sugar, crushed ice cubes, chilled water, bhang powder and rose essence.
Step 2: Stir for a minute and transfer it into a blender and beat till it is frothy.
Step 3: Pour bhang lassi in a glass and add sour cream on top. Serve chilled.

The Red Emperor

"Forget it Joe, It's Chinatown"

JERRY BADER

THE GIFT

Beverly Hills Shopping District, Rodeo Drive

A large black limousine pulls up and parks under the "No Parking Anytime" sign in front of the Three Kings Tailor Shop. A beat cop on his rounds notices the car but keeps on walking past as if it's invisible. In the front seat is a driver dressed in a black suit, white shirt, and black tie with a *Guan Yu* stickpin. In the back is Benson Yeung, an elderly Chinese gentlemen, wearing a beautiful, charcoal pinstripe bespoke suit, a crisp white shirt, red silk tie, and a *Guan Yu* stickpin.

The driver gets out of the car buttoning his jacket to hide the Smith & Wesson Bodyguard® 380. He proceeds to the rear passenger door and opens it. The elderly white-haired man slowly exits the automobile carrying a black ebony cane with a gold dragon's head handle in one hand, and a small shiny red bag overflowing with gold tissue paper in the other.

The two men enter the Three Kings. It's a well-appointed shop with bolts of expensive fabric lining the walls, and mahogany wood paneling displaying numerous Hirschfeld-esk caricatures of famous clients. Mo Fields, the owner, is seated at a large mahogany partner's desk at the far end of the showroom doing paper work; his six-year-old daughter Betty is seated opposite reading Roald Dahl's 'The BFG.'

Betty turns to see who's entered. As soon as she realizes who it is, she jumps up and runs to the old man, clutching his well-tailored leg as if it was a prize possession. Her father smiles at his daughter's reaction. He gets up to greet the old man. The little girl notices the red bag and points.

Betty: "For me?"

Yeung: "Patience little one, patience..." The old man goes to hand the little girl the bag but stops.

Yeung: "Do not open it until I tell you. Understand?" The little girl bobs her head up and down.

Yeung: "Now go and read your book, while I talk to your Father." The little girl snatches the red bag from the old man and hurries back to the desk with her mysterious package. Too excited to read, she just stares at the bag as if staring will reveal its contents.

The driver moves to the door scanning the street for anything that looks suspicious. What he doesn't notice is the shabby little man with the big hat in the window of the Starbucks across the street. A more attentive bodyguard would have noticed the man in the Borsalino was far more interested in what was happening in the Three Kings than he was in the morning edition of the LA Times.

Fields and the old man move off to one side as if they're selecting fabric for a new suit. The old man takes a photograph of four men out of his jacket pocket and points to the one man who's Chinese.

Yeung: "That one. Tonight."

Fields takes the photograph and looks at it carefully, imprinting the man's face in his memory. "What about the others?"

The others are: a grossly overweight fat man in a grey three-piece suit, a bug-eye fop with a white silk puff hankie overflowing the pocket of his tuxedo, and a creepy little thug wearing a shabby suit and a Borsalino that all but covers his face.

Yeung: "Just the one, he's the "*Pantu*"... the traitor. The others are "*Shagua*"... fools"

Fields nods and hands the photograph back to the old man who slips it back into his pocket. He takes his hand out holding a stickpin in the shape of a Blue Chinese Lantern.

Yeung: "Make sure you wear this."

Fields acknowledges the instructions and takes the talisman. The old man turns to see the little girl looking intently at the red bag. She senses his conversation with her father is finished and turns to look.

Yeung: "Now little one, your patience is rewarded."

The little girl grabs the red package pulling what seems like an endless supply of gold tissue paper from the bag. She reaches in and pulls out a brightly painted statue of a fierce looking Chinese warrior. The eight-inch figure has a red face, long beard, and green robe wrapping around ornate body armor. He's carrying a long-handled weapon with a crescent-bladed battle-axe spewing from the mouth of a jade-headed dragon. The statue makes an odd clinking sound as if partially filled with pebbles as the little girl waves her new prized possession in the air.

Betty: "It's beautiful Uncle!" She calls him Uncle out of respect and love.

Yeung: "You keep this on your desk for good luck. *Guan Yu* will protect you, so keep him close. Understand?"

Betty: "Yes Uncle I understand, I love him. I'll call him Red Face. How do you say Red Face in Chinese?"

Yeung: "His name is *Guan Yu*, but you can call him *Mian Chi*, Red Face. Now go and pick out a nice fabric for me."

The little girl jumps from her chair and runs to a shelf holding bolts of the most expensive Vicuna fabric in the shop. Her father laughs. The old man turns to Fields… "You've taught her well. Make one charcoal and one black. And don't forget the surgeon's cuffs."

Betty carefully places the statue on the desk. She imagines a time when the exotic warrior with the red face lived, and wonders what kind of adventures he must have experienced.

The old man finishes his business with Mo Fields, kisses the little girl on the head and leaves. The man in the hat exits the coffee shop, and casually strolls by the window of the high-end tailor as if he was in the market for a badly needed new suit; but haberdashery was the last thing on his mind.

THE HIT

Green Dragon Restaurant

Mo Fields walks into the Green Dragon Restaurant. The Dragon is safe territory controlled by Benson Yeung and his "*Hong Mian Gang.*" It's Friday night and the place is hopping with an assortment of Chinese gangsters, movie executives, and the occasional misplaced civilian. At one table is Benson Yeung, his two sons and their wives.

At another are ex-gangster Arnie Bernardo, his wife, Lonnie, his two closest associates Vito Fanucci and Sid Paletta, and their current live-in girlfriends.

An odd group of misfits are sitting at a table situated next to the entrance to the kitchen. Four men occupy the table: a fat man overflowing his three-piece suit as he ostentatiously pats the sweat from his brow; a vaguely effeminate dandy with bulging eyes in a dark suit with a white silk hankie spilling out of his breast pocket; a scruffy gunsel who doesn't bother to remove his oversized fedora; and a thirty-something Chinese man in a trendy suit and spiked hair.

A beautiful young Chinese woman with a short-cropped Vidal Sassoon haircut approaches Fields. Sally Yang is as exotic as she is beautiful. She wears a long high-necked, gold silk cheongsam with a green dragon wrapping gracefully around her breasts and backside. The dress features a teasingly sensual slit up the side, almost to her hip, revealing a long lovely leg balanced on a shiny green spiked high heel.

Yang: "Good evening, sir. A table for one?"

Working for Benson Yeung taught Yang to pay attention to details like the working cuffs on the man's suit jacket:

a sartorial refinement that denoted a well heeled man of good taste. Fields raises his hand as if to wipe an imaginary piece of lint from his jacket. The woman immediately spots the Blue Lantern stickpin in his lapel.

Fields: "I'm meeting some friends."

Yang bows gracefully, if not solicitously, allowing him to pass. Fields quickly spots his man at a table strategically placed near the entrance to the kitchen. He reaches into his jacket for the Glock 30S as he briskly walks toward the table. The target is sitting with his back to the wall. As he passes the table he slows, just long enough for the man to notice, he raises the Glock and pulls the trigger.

BANG!

A bright red hole appears in the man's forehead; his brains are splattered all over the gold and green wallpaper.

Fields doesn't stop but keeps on moving out the door, through the crowded steamy kitchen with a dozen Chinese cooks all yelling at each other in Cantonese. Fields exits the back door, gets into the stolen car provided for him by Benson Yeung's driver, and disappears into the night before anyone in the restaurant understands exactly what has happened. It's all over in less than three minutes.

THE AFTERMATH

Green Dragon Restaurant

A large crowd has gathered outside the Green Dragon Restaurant, drawn to the confusion like pyromaniacs to a fire. The parasitic press has swooped in like vultures picking at the entrails of a voyeuristic mob with nothing better to do on a Friday night than to try and insert themselves into the evening news.

A few may even be lucky enough to grab a macabre selfie with Peter Pretty Boy Chen's body bag, as it's taken to the ME's bus for the trip to the morgue. One frenzied, Botoxed female reporter sticks a microphone in the faces of Detectives Grist and Dime as they brush past into the restaurant.

Crime scene techs are gathered around the table near the kitchen entrance. Half the customers are complaining about not being allowed to go home while the other half are excited about the evening's improvised entertainment. Sitting quietly in the corner are Arnie and Lonnie Bernardo and their associates. Grist and Dime approach.

Grist: "Jesus Christ Bernardo, you should consider staying home for dinner once in a while. There always seems to be a dead body around whenever you go out."

Bernardo: "Hi Joe, Velma, how you been?"

Grist: "Better than the poor schmuck whose brains are all over the wallpaper."

Dime: "Anybody see anything?"

Vito: "The guy was a pro. He was in and out of here before anybody knew what was happening."

Bernardo: "He kept his head down and his back to almost everyone."

Lonnie: "He was well dressed I can tell you that. The suit he was wearing didn't come off the rack... maybe Sally saw his face."

Dime: "Sally?"

Lonnie: "The hostess in the gold dress..."

One of Benson's Yeung's sons approaches the detectives.

Henry Yeung: "Excuse me detectives but my father is an old man and we have young children at home."

Grist: "Velma, go speak to Mr. Yeung and then let him and his family go home."

Henry Yeung: "Thank you..." Henry goes back to where his family is sitting and tells them one of the detectives will be right over.

Grist: "Velma, the old man must have known the stiff. Find out who he was but don't push it, he's not going to give up anything here. We'll go after him in private. And tell Alvarez to get the hostess's statement; she must have seen the shooter come in."

Dime nods. She deliver's her partner's instructions to Alvarez and then goes to question the Yeungs. Grist turns back to Bernardo and his group. "Any of you know the stiff?"

Vito: "Must have been one of Yeung's boys or a civilian. None of the other Chinese crews would dare pull a stunt like this, especially in Yeung's own restaurant."

Grist: "What about the people he was with?"

Bernardo laughs. "A real odd bunch… something out of Dashiell Hammett."

Grist: "Okay, thanks, you guys can go home, and for god's sake Lonnie learn to cook… I've got enough open cases; I don't need any more dead bodies."

Bernardo and his group leave while Grist heads on over to interview the fat man and his friends.

THE PLAYERS

Police Squad Room

Grist and Dime are sitting at their desks facing each other while Alvarez is standing leaning against a file cabinet sipping a cup of coffee.

Grist: "Okay, what have we got?" Each of them starts leafing through their notes.

Alvarez: " Sally Yang, the hostess, says she didn't notice the guy's face… She did notice his suit, said it had surgeon's cuffs, whatever they are?"

Grist: "I'll buy you a copy of Esquire… surgeon's cuffs are working buttons on the sleeve. Military surgeons wore them so they could roll-up their sleeves when operating in the field. You generally only see them on expensive custom-made suits."

Dime: "Well ain't you the fashionista…"

Alvarez: "He was Caucasian, she thinks, but couldn't or wouldn't describe him."

Grist: "Yeah, all us white boys look alike."

Dime: "Old man Yeung says he didn't know the guy, but his son, Henry, said the stiff was one of their drivers, Peter Chen. Had a rap sheet but nothing major, just kid stuff, stealing cars, that kind of thing. Street name, Peter Pretty Boy Chen; I guess he never saw a mirror he didn't like."

Grist: "Any reason to think the old man had him killed?"

Dime: "Too low level for him to know anything the old man would be concerned about."

Alvarez: "Hard to say, the triads have their rules. You fuckup and you'll find yourself splattered all over somebody's wallpaper. It's Chinatown."

Dime: "Not in his own place… that would be kind of crazy."

Grist: "Maybe not… the old bastard is one smart fortune cookie. He didn't get to be Dragon Head by playing nice… he earned that gold dragon-headed walking stick. And there's plenty of blood on it from what I've heard."

Dime: "What about Huey, Dewey, and Louie?"

Grist: "Jesus, that sideshow… The fat man is one Cyrus Green. Says he's in import/export and the other two are his associates. The dandy with the silk hankie is Zoltan Monaco… talking to him made me want to take a shower. And the shabby punk with the big hat is Wilbur Krook… appears to be the muscle based on the bulge in his jacket."

Alvarez: "So how does Pretty Boy figure in to this?"

Dime: "He was their driver."

Alvarez: "One of the Yeung's must have had some business with these guys."

Grist: "I think it's time we turned up the heat on the Yeung family."

AN EXOTIC DISH

Bobby Bloom's Montmartre Gallery Bistro

The restaurant is an eclectic combination of Rennie Mackintosh furniture and paintings used for pulp fiction movie posters. Leon Bailey, a tall, elegantly dressed coffee-colored gentleman, stands at a podium-style desk taking reservations on the phone in his deep baritone Jamaican accent.

Sally Yang dressed in the latest trendy styles right out of one of those Japanese fashion magazines enters the stained glass doors and approaches Bailey.

Bailey: "Can I help you?"

Yang: "I'd like to speak with Mr. Bloom, please."

Bailey: "He's not here right now, but I expect him back any minute."

Yang: "Can I wait?"

Bailey: "You can wait at the bar. I'll have someone bring you some coffee, if you like?" She nods approval and heads for the bar. Bailey, signals a waiter to get the young woman some coffee, then goes back to recording reservations in his large ledger-style appointment book.

Five minutes later a short, balding, spark plug of a man with a neatly trimmed grey beard, dapperly attired in a charcoal grey turtleneck, and black bespoke suit, enters.

Bailey says a few words to the man who glances in Yang's direction. Yang is sitting at the bar in her short red leather skirt, and black leather bolero jacket, daintily sipping coffee from a China cup. The man approaches Yang. He speaks with a refined French accent.

Bloom: "I'm Bobby Bloom… You wanted to speak to me?"

She reaches into her red and black designer purse and pulls out a thick envelope and hands it to Bloom. He looks the woman in the eye trying to get a fix on what this is all about. Bloom opens the envelope crammed with hundred-dollar bills and two photographs. He pulls out the photographs and places them on the bar beside the envelope: one of the photos is of a *Guan Yu* statue about eight inches high, the other is of Peter Pretty Boy Chen.

Yang: "I'm Sally Yang, and I work at the Green Dragon. You must have heard about the murder at the Dragon."

Bloom: "You could hardly avoid hearing about it. It's been on the news non-stop since it happened."

She points to the photographs of Peter Chen and the *Guan Yu* statue. "The man killed was my fiancé, Peter Chen. He gave me that statue for an engagement gift. It's all I have left of him and it's been stolen. I want it back! She points to the envelope. Bloom notices she's not wearing an engagement ring.

Yang: "That's $5,000… I'd like to hire you to find the statute, and whoever killed Peter."

Bloom: "Young lady, I run a restaurant. You need the police, not a restaurateur."

Yang: "Mr. Bloom, please… I work for Benson Yeung… I know exactly who you are, and what you do? The police have little interest in a man like Peter, and no interest at all in my little memento."

Bloom takes the two photographs and sticks them back into the envelope with the cash. He looks at the pretty porcelain doll of a woman sitting in front of him.

Bloom: "Was the statue of value?"

Yang: "Sentimental value only... And perhaps superstition... Chinatown is filled with cheap *Guan Yu* statues but only that one was given to me by Peter. It's bad luck to lose a *Brother of The Peach Orchard*. I must have it back, I must!"

Bloom doesn't believe a word she says. If she worked for Benson Yeung, she and her dead boyfriend could be neck deep in something nasty.

The exotic Sally Yang in her tight red leather skirt reminded Bloom of the poisonous Oleander, beautiful to look at, but deadly to even be near. That said he was tempted, not so much by the 5K but rather by the intrigue, something he sorely missed since leaving the French DGSE.

What the hell, maybe his girlfriend, the delicious Detective Velma Dime could point him in the right direction.

Bloom stuffs the envelope into the inside breast pocket of his cashmere and wool suit jacket, making sure Yang catches a glimpse of the Barak SP-21 resting in his black leather shoulder holster.

Bloom: "All right Miss Yang, I'll give you a week to see what I can dig up."

She slides off the bar stool with the grace of a Tsushima leopard and kisses him on the cheek.

Yang: "Thank you Bobby, this means a lot to me."

This was a woman who was not afraid to use her exotic looks and sex appeal to get what she wanted, but Bloom was used to danger, and the women who came along with it.

TOO LITTLE TOO LATE

The Montmartre Gallery Bistro

The restaurant is packed. Bobby Bloom is sitting at the bar having a drink with his girlfriend Velma Dime. Leon Bailey the Jamaican *maitre d*, and Bloom's best undercover operative, is talking to an overly excited little man with big bulging eyes, waving a white silk hankie in the air. The odd little man hands the tall Jamaican a business card. Bailey says something that appears to appease him. Bailey turns and heads to where Bloom and Dime are sitting.

Bailey: "Boss, the fellow in the corner insists on speaking with you." Bailey hands Bloom the card, *Professor Zoltan Monaco, Historical Artifact Consultant*. Bloom looks at the card and hands it to his girlfriend. Dime looks across the room and sees the funny little man staring at them.

Dime: "Bobby, that guy was at the *Dragon* when Chen got whacked. He was sitting at the same table."

Bloom: "Interesting... Listen, you're not going to like this, but I need you to keep your cool."

Dime: "Why? What's up?"

Bloom: "Sally Yang hired me to look into Peter Chen's murder..."

Dime: "What the fuck Bobby! You know that's my case..."

The dandy in the corner loses his patience. He tosses his linen napkin onto the table with an effeminate flourish; gets up, and heads for the bar where Bloom and Dime are sitting.

He speaks in some kind of whiny, indiscernible European accent. He is so intent on getting Bloom's attention that he doesn't recognize Dime as one of the detectives that worked the Peter Chen crime scene.

Monaco hands Bloom another of his cards. "Excuse me young lady, but I must speak to Mr. Bloom in private. It's an urgent matter of extreme delicacy." Dime gives Bloom a look that says, *don't you dare.*

Bloom: "You can speak in front of my associate. I'll vouch for her..."

Monaco: "Well, if you insist but understand... discretion is extremely important. I'd like to hire you to find an object of great historical significance." Monaco reaches into his jacket and pulls out a photograph, but before he gets a chance to show it, Bloom responds.

Bloom: "That wouldn't happen to be a photograph of an eight-inch *Guan Yu* statue, would it?"

The odd little man with the Marty Feldman eyes almost pops a blood vessel. Dime takes the opportunity to snatch the photograph from Monaco's hand. He's startled.

Monaco: "You know about the statue?"

Bloom: "It seems everyone wants to get their hands on that little guy. In fact, I already have a client interested in obtaining it."

Monaco: "That bitch! That double-crossing bitch... I'll double whatever she's paying."

Bloom: "What make's you think it's a she?"

Monaco: "Yeung? Is it Benson Yeung?"

Bloom: "Sorry Professor, that's privileged information."
Frustrated Monaco grabs the photograph out of Dime's
hand.

Monaco: "You'll be hearing from my associates, Mr.
Bloom. They don't like being denied."

Dime: "Listen you little weasel, do you have any idea who
you're threatening?"

Monaco: "Has-been spooks don't scare us young lady."
Dime reaches into her purse so Monaco can catch a
glimpse of the 9mm Glock resting under her gold
detective's shield.

Dime: "Think again asshole!"

A light goes on in the little man's head as he realizes the
sexy lady in the skin-tight dress is one of the detectives
from the Green Dragon.

Monaco: "You're the cop from the other night… the one
talking to the Yeungs."

Dime: "Get the fuck out of here before I arrest you for
disturbing my peace…"

Monaco is so upset he stomps off leaving the restaurant
without finishing his meal, or paying his bill. Bailey looks
back at Bloom, who just shakes his head as if to say, *let
him go*. Dime feels the flush of red rising up from her
chest to her cheeks. She looks at the Frenchman with fire
in her eyes.

Dime: "So I'm your associate? You'll vouch for me?
You got to be fucking kidding?"

Bloom: "Relax. You would never have learned anything from him without our little charade."

Dime: "I better call Joe." Dime takes the cell phone out of her purse to call her partner.

Dime: "I swear Bobby, if those clowns don't kill you. I will... Joe, its Velma, you'll never guess what just happened..."

THE SURGEON'S CUFF

Benson Yeung's Office

Grist and Dime are seated in a matching pair of black lacquer Shanghai Art Déco side chairs, with red silk cushions and gold trim. Benson Yeung is relaxed behind a matching desk, with his son Henry, standing arms crossed in front of a series of Zhang Yuan flower paintings. On the desk directly in front of Grist and Dime is an eight-inch statue of *Guan Yu*.

Grist: "Mr. Yeung, can you tell us why Peter Chen was sitting with Cyrus Green and his associates the night he was murdered."

Dime: "Peter Chen worked for you, isn't that right?"

Henry Yeung steps forward to answer, but his father raises his hand to stop him. Grist notices that the buttons on the sleeve of the old man's suit jacket are undone so the sleeve can be rolled up.

Yeung: "My son is very protective of an old man, but he was correct when he told you that Peter was just a driver."

Grist: "And Mr. Green?"

Yeung: "Mr. Green came to me wanting to buy an ancient artifact that his associate, Professor Monaco, told him I owned. He was very persistent, but mistaken. To appease Mr. Green, I offered Peter as a driver to show him around Chinatown. I even invited him and his friends to dinner as a show of friendship."

Dime: "He wanted the *Guan Yu* statue?"

Yeung: "Yes my dear, *Guan Yu*. Chinatown has many such statues. You can see them in the window of almost every business. He is the Lord of Prosperity and Commerce, but I knew Mr. Green wouldn't find the statue he was looking for."

Grist: "And why not?"

The old man smiles. "Because Detective Grist, it doesn't exist. It's a legend, a fairy tale; a made-up story to tell children at bedtime."

Dime: "This Green fellow seems to think it exists."

Grist: "And he's pretty sure you have it."

The old man is starting to get irritated by the prolonged interrogation. "Let me speak plainly detectives. You know who I am. The fat man and his silly little friends are fools. Avaricious fools.

You see... legend has it that when *The Three Brothers of the Peach Orchard* made their pact to restore the Han Dynasty, they celebrated by creating three beautiful statues: one in each of their images: the *Guan Yu* was filled with red rubies, the *Zang Fei* with green emeralds, and the *Lui Bei* with precious diamonds.

Each statue symbolized leadership of one of the *Three Kingdoms*, the alliance created to restore the Han. Whoever possessed one of these statues controlled the associated Kingdom.

There are those who believe these statues exist, and whoever possesses one, has the right to lead one of the three powerful Chinese brotherhoods."

Grist: "You're talking about the triads."

Yeung: "With all due respect, Detective, I can't expect you to understand two thousand years of Chinese culture and history. I assure you, I am just a humble businessman.

I am successful and old, and people come to me with their problems. I try my best to provide guidance, but that is all there is to it.

The story of *Guan Yu* and the ruby-filled statue is just that: a story, a folk tale for children, and ignorant, greedy fools like Mr. Green and his friends. He is searching for something that does not exist." The old man is worn-out from telling the story. His son sees that his father has had enough.

Henry: "I'm afraid you'll have to leave. My father is tired. You can find *Guan Yu* statues in every shop window… you can buy them in any Chinese gift shop, but none of them will have anything inside but candy."

Dime: "Candy?"

The old man takes his gold Dragon-headed cane and pushes the *Guan Yu* statue that's on his desk in Dime's direction.

Yeung: "A gift from an old man to a pretty lady…"

Dime: "Sir, I can't accept a gift."

Yeung: "Please I insist, after all, *Guan Yu* is known to be the Protector of the Police, besides there are a lot more where that came from."

Dime picks up the statue and looks at it closely. Yeung opens the bottom drawer of his desk, reaches down and pulls out an exact replica of the *Guan Yu* he just gave Dime.

Yeung: "Trinkets my dear, bought and sold by the hundreds. Give it a twist."

Dime doesn't quite understand. "A twist?"

Yeung: "Yes, it comes apart at the chest. Perhaps you'll find *Hong bao*, a red treasure."

Dime does as she is told, twisting the upper body of the figure until it comes apart. She removes the top half exposing a stash of red cinnamon candies called Imperials.

Yeung: "You see my dear, in Chinatown: things are not always what they appear to be."

Grist and Dime leave Yeung's office with Dime holding the *Guan Yu*. On the way out, Grist stops at the desk of Yeung's secretary.

Grist: "Excuse me..."

I couldn't help but notice Mr. Yeung's suit, it was very nice. I happen to be in the market for a nice suit like that. Perhaps you can tell me who Mr. Yeung's tailor is?"

The pretty young Chinese secretary opens a drawer in her desk and hands Grist a card.

Mo Fields
Gentlemen's Bespoke Tailor
Rodeo Drive, Beverly Hills, CA
By Appointment Only

Back in Yeung's office the old man hands his son the *Guan Yu* statue he just put on his desk.

Yeung: "Meet with Fields and make the exchange."

YANG'S YEN

Bobby Bloom's Townhouse

Bobby Bloom pulls into the garage of his luxury townhouse. On the seat beside him is a DVD copy of the surveillance footage showing Peter Chen stealing a *Guan Yu* statue from Yeung's desk, probably one filled with candy, a deadly mistake that got him killed.

Bloom figured a thousand dollars cash would be just the right incentive needed to pry-loose the phantom evidence from Yeung's secretary. Bloom picks up the disk, slips it in his pocket, and enters the townhouse.

Once inside, Bloom takes off his jacket, pours himself a Brandy, and flops down on the couch, ready to watch the DVD. Staring back at him from the coffee table is a *Guan Yu* statue. Sitting underneath the statue is a note.

Yeung's secretary has just been pulled out of the lake. I can't find Joe. Have him meet me if he calls. Enjoy the tchotchke. I'll explain when I get home... Love V.

The doorbell rings. Bloom sticks the note in his pocket and goes to the door to see the lovely porcelain face of Sally Yang looking back through the window. He opens the door.

Bloom: "Miss Yang, how nice to see you."

Sally Yang takes a quick look behind her to see if anyone has followed and then enters the townhouse. She follows Bloom into the living room where she spots the *Guan Yu* sitting on the coffee table beside Bloom's snifter of brandy.

Bloom: "Can I get you a drink? Brandy?"

She nods yes. Bloom walks to the bar and pours a drink
for Yang. When he turns around Yang is seated in one of
two matching black and chrome Le Corbusier chairs
with the *Guan Yu* in one hand, and a Walther PK380 in
the other.

Yang: "I believe this is mine."

Bloom moves to the matching Le Corbusier couch, picks
up his brandy, swirls it around the over-sized glass,
shrugs, and takes a sip.

Bloom: "You got what you wanted; I've been paid, so why
the gun?"

Yang: "Just making sure we don't have a problem."

Bloom: "You'll have no problem with me, Miss Yang. I
can't speak for Benson Yeung and Sons, but not with me."

Yang: "How did you get it?"

Bloom: "I get paid to solve problems, not to report how I
do it. You have what you came for, so I suggest you
disappear, before you suffer the same fate as your phony
fiancé."

Sally Yang gets up and moves to the front of the
townhouse. As she gets to the door, she turns, still
holding both the statue and the Walther.

Yang: "Are we good?"

Bloom: "We're good, Miss Yang... good as two people like
us can be."
Sally Yang opens the door and leaves. Bloom goes back to
his Bauhaus decorated living room, drops down into the

soft as butter leather, and takes another sip of brandy. After a moment savoring the rich warm elixir as it slides down his throat, he picks up his phone to call Dime.

Bloom: "Velma, you okay..."

Dime: "Yeah, I'm good, but this poor girl has a hole in the back of her pretty head."

Bloom: "Are you sure it's Yeung's secretary?"

Dime: "It's her..."

Bloom: "*Merde*... That's too bad."

Dime: "We found a thousand dollars in her purse... a bit soggy but... you wouldn't happen to know anything about it, would you?"

Bloom ignores the question. "Listen I have good news and bad news... I know why Peter Chen got whacked, and probably who's responsible."

Dime: "Uh-huh... and the bad news?"

Bloom: "Your little *Guan* is gone." The only response is laughter.

THE EXCHANGE

The Three Kings Tailor Shop

Wilbur Krook taps on the window of the big black limousine parked in front of the Three Kings tailor shop. As the irritated driver lowers the window, Krook hits him square in the face with the set of brass knuckles on his right hand. The driver slumps down on the seat, unconscious, blood trickling from his broken nose onto the black leather seat.

Krook enters the shop with his hand wrapped around the SIG Mosquito in the pocket of his shabby suit-jacket. Six-year-old Betty Fields is sitting at her father's desk with a large box of crayons obscuring her *Guan Yu* statue. A coloring book is open in front of her along with an assortment of colored drawing pencils.

Henry Yeung and Mo Fields are off to the side in deep conversation. Krook focuses on Yeung and Fields, ignoring the little girl. Henry Yeung's back is to Krook while he talks to Mo Fields who is holding a *Guan Yu* statue. Fields spots Krook.

Krook: "I'll relieve you fellows of that little souvenir."

Yeung turns around to face Krook who's holding the SIG Mosquito equipped with a silencer.

Yeung: "Be careful little man, you really don't want to do this."

Fields catches his daughter's attention. Betty grabs her *Guan Yu* and hides under the desk as her father moves for his Glock 30S hidden behind a bolt of navy blue cashmere and wool.
POP! POP!

Krook fires two shots: the first one hits Yeung in the shoulder knocking him backwards into the corner of the mahogany partner's desk. He falls to the floor, unconscious, with blood oozing from the contusion caused by the corner of the desk. A red stain spreads across the front of his crisp white custom-made shirt from the bullet that just ripped through his shoulder.

The second shot hits Fields in the side as he reaches for the Glock causing him to fall forward banging his head on the side of the shelf holding the expensive bolts of fabric.

Betty leaves her *Guan Yu* hidden under the desk and runs to her father ignoring the danger. Krook quickly moves to where Fields dropped the statue he was holding. He picks it up just as Betty attacks his leg kicking and screaming bloody murder.

Krook tries to secure the statue as he desperately attempts to shake the little girl from his leg. The door to the Three Kings flies open as Joe Grist hurls himself into the showroom diving for cover behind an ornate carved chair reserved for frustrated wives and impatient mistresses.

Grist: "LA Police!! Drop the gun!"

With his left hand still holding the prized *Guan Yu* statue, Krook grabs the little girl under her arm. He raises her up off the ground so that she covers most of his vital organs. He still has the SIG Mosquito in his right hand.

Krook: "I don't want to hurt the girl but I'll shoot her if you don't drop your gun."
Grist raises his hands and stands up, now only half shielded by the elaborately carved chair. Betty is

wiggling and squirming as much as she can; her legs are kicking wildly and her arms and elbows are a blur of flailing confusion.

Krook attempts to secure his hold on the little girl but she kicks him in the crotch with the heel of her shoe while simultaneously catching him in the left eye with one of her pointed little elbows.

Krook lets out a pathetic groan as he doubles over in pain. He drops to one knee letting go of the little girl just as Grist fires spinning the shabby little gunsel around. Grist runs to the child, and with one motion sweeps her off the Persian carpet, and deposits her under the partner's desk. He turns around to focus his attention on Krook and his SIG Mosquito, but he's gone along with the *Guan Yu* that Mo Fields dropped.

The door to the sewing room is open. Grist takes off after the little thug. He zigzags his way around a series of industrial sewing machines, mannequins with half-finished suits, and cutting tables piled high with bolts of fabric.

The back door flings open and Krook makes a run for it. By the time Grist gets to the alley all he sees is the face of the shabby little man in the big hat staring back at him from the rear seat of a silver Chevy as it disappears into traffic.

Grist hears the sound of police sirens and screeching tires coming from the front of the shop. As he re-enters the showroom, he sees Dime holding the girl. Various paramedics tend to Fields and Yeung. Outside, Yeung's driver is sitting on the back of an ambulance being looked after by another paramedic.
Dime puts the little girl down so she can give her father a kiss before they take him out to one of the waiting

ambulances. Henry Yeung is the next to be carried out to join Fields on the trip to the hospital.

Dime: "Are you okay Joe?"

Grist: "Yeah, just mad I didn't catch the little punk."

Dime: "We'll get him Joe. You can count on that."

Grist: "He got away with the statue..."

Betty: "Not mine, I hid it."

Grist and Dime look at the little girl who's holding her *Guan Yu*.

Dime: "I guess it's true what Yeung said..."

Grist: "He said a lot of stuff..."

Dime: "You don't remember, him telling us *Guan Yu* is the protector of all policemen?"

Betty: "Uncle Yeung says he's good luck."

Betty goes over to the exhausted Joe Grist who bends down on one knee so he can be at Betty's eye level.

Betty: "*Mian Chi* saved your life, and you saved mine. Now he's yours."

The little girl hands Grist the statue and kisses the handsome cop on the cheek. Dime and Grist both smile.

Grist: "I can't accept your good luck charm."

Betty: "You must, that's the way things are done."

Dime: "Who told you that?"

Betty: "Uncle Yeung. He would be very angry with me if I didn't do the honorable thing."

Grist graciously accepts the little girl's gift, as the woman from Child Services shows up to take care of Betty until her father is out of the hospital.

THE GANG
THAT COULDN'T SHOOT STRAIGHT

A Seedy Hotel Somewhere in Chinatown

Cyrus Green, Zoltan Monaco, Wilbur Krook, and Sally Yang all stand around a table dejectedly looking down at what they've manage to acquire.

On the table are two *Guan Yu* statues that they've hammer to pieces, not knowing that they could have simply twisted them open. Spread out on the table amongst the shards of broken colored clay are little red cinnamon candies called Imperials.

Monaco turns to Krook and slaps him across the face. He speaks in his unrecognizable whiny foreign accent. "You Fool! You stupid fool! It's candy, cheap dime store candy."

Krook grabs Monaco by the collar and starts to shake him like a rag doll.

Yang: "Will you two shut the fuck up?"

The two men stop their squabbling at the sound of the china doll's obscenity. Monaco turns his wrath on Yang. "You should talk… your brilliant boyfriend stole the first worthless piece of junk. And you, you silly bitch, blew $5,000 on fifty cents worth of candy."

She looks at Cyrus Green. "What the hell are we going to do now? Peter is dead. The cops are looking for Wilbur. I can't go back to the *Dragon*. This whole thing has been a disaster from the start."

Green places his hands in the pockets of the oversized waistcoat that wraps around his massive extended belly. He chuckles several times almost to himself; more for affect than from humor. He speaks in a pompous, overly formal style. "Well, well, isn't this a pickle? A pickle of mass proportions I think. [chuckle] Cheap dime store candies indeed. That is what we've acquired, garish little red cinnamon treats. [chuckle]

Well my friends we've been royally duped by the powers that be. The enigmatic Benson Yeung has played us for fools this time, but like the Phoenix we shall rise again."

Yang: "What the hell are you talking about? We'll all end up like Peter if we're ever spotted by Yeung's people. And you know they're out there just waiting for us to pop our heads up."

Green: "Now, now, my lovely, don't worry your pretty little head. There are three precious statues out there, each one owned by a different Dragon, each eager to gain control over the others. A deal can be had, a deal can always be had... After all, my dear: this is Chinatown."

EPILOGUE
'Forget It Joe, It's Chinatown'

Police Squad Room

Detective Velma Dime is sitting at her desk doing paper work. Alvarez is at the coffee machine staring at an empty pot as if the coffee disappeared by magic.

Joe Grist comes into the squad room after a couple of days off. Alvarez turns around waving the empty coffee pot in the air. He notices Dime sipping coffee from her official blue LA Homicide mug.

Alvarez: "You know everyone, and that includes you Detective Dime, whoever takes the last cup is supposed to make a fresh pot."

Grist: "Don't look at me. I haven't been here for two days."

Dime takes the final swig of her coffee. "You're a cop Alvarez, you want to accuse me of something, you need evidence."

Grist: "How ya do'in gorgeous? I missed that smartass mouth of yours."

Dime: "Glad to have you back partner. Alvarez has been a real pain in the ass to work with."

Alvarez turns from his coffee-making duties. "I heard that Velma..."

Grist notices the *Guan Yu* statue that Betty Fields gave him sitting on the edge of his desk. He picks up the souvenir and holds it up for Alvarez.

Grist: "We haven't got coffee, but we got delicious little red candies."

Alvarez: "Forget it, those red Imperials will burn the roof of your mouth. You won't be able taste anything for a week."

Grist starts to twist the upper body of the statue to open it. "How about it Velma, you like them little and hot."

Dime: "Don't think I won't tell Bobby you said that. And those candies… they're all yours."

Grist takes the top half of the *Guan Yu* statue and places it on his desk. He peers into the bottom expecting to see little red cinnamon treats. Instead of small red candies, the bottom of the statue is filled with multi-caret-sized rubies.

Grist: "Velma you sure you don't want some of these."

Dime shakes her head. "No thanks Joe. Enjoy."

Grist: "Well partner… I'll save you some. You never know when they might come in handy." Grist puts the top of *Guan Yu* back on the statue. "This has been some crazy case. I just get the feeling that we haven't heard the end of it."

Dime: "Forget it Joe, it's Chinatown."

THE END

The Redhead

Rip-Off

The Art Of The Grift

JERRY BADER

PROLOGUE

Gustav Klimt was a successful Austrian artist specializing in exotic figurative paintings and drawings during the pinnacle of Austrian culture around the *fin de siècle*. Despite his success, Klimt's career was not without controversy. An early commission for the Great Hall of the University of Vienna became a turning point in his career. The three paintings he produced for the university, *Philosophy*, *Medicine*, and *Jurisprudence* where dubbed pornographic and were never displayed on the ceiling of the Great Hall as originally intended. Klimt would never again accept a public commission, and instead relied upon wealthy, culturally sophisticated female patrons. Many if not most of his patrons and models were Jewish, despite the fact he himself was raised Catholic; as a consequence, many of his paintings were confiscated by the Nazis during WWII. In 1945 with the war coming to an end, retreating SS forces set fire to the Immendorf Castle were many of Klimt's masterpieces were being kept.

Klimt was by all accounts an eccentric genius who when painting dressed in a long smock with nothing on underneath. Even during portrait sessions with wealthy female patrons, he would disappear into another room where he enjoyed the companionship of the two or three semi-naked models that seemed to be constantly lounging close at hand. Klimt never married, but he did father several children from his liaisons with his models. Although the names of almost all his models have been lost forever, one particular favorite has survived, a beautiful Bohemian redhead by the name of Hilde Roth who appears in several of Klimt's most familiar masterpieces. Whatever happened to Fraulein Roth remains a mystery.

THE BAIT

Scarborough, Ontario, Canada, a run-of-the-mill office complex, one of those places that supply phone service and meeting rooms for start-ups without the capital to rent full-time office space. The building is located across the road from a Chinese mall that rents small stalls to businesses specializing in selling knockoff purses, pirated DVDs, and articles of clothing that would make an over-hyped pop star blush.

A beautiful redhead gets off the elevator and heads down the hallway looking for the door with a sign that reads "Lucky Eight Casting." The sign is hand-written in an overly elaborate script, thumb-tacked to the door with a large red pushpin. The woman's mobile phone vibrates.

Helen: "Hello"

Voice on the phone: "Have you had the meeting?"

Helen: "No, not yet. I'm just going in now."

Voice on the phone: "Honey, there's still time to back out. No amount of money is worth seeing you get hurt."

Helen: "Don't worry… I can look after myself. I have to go and don't call me again. We'll have plenty of time to talk when this is over."

Voice on the phone: "Okay, but please be careful… I hear the freight elevator… I better hang up."

Helen: "Get rid of your phone's SIM card just in case, and I'll do the same."
Both parties hang up. Helen takes the SIM card out of her phone, drops it on the floor, and steps on it hard with her

high heel. She picks up the pieces and sticks them in her purse to be disposed of later.

Helen enters finding six metal chairs, five of them filled with attractive redheads. Helen takes the last empty chair and waits. At the opposite end of the room is a two-way mirrored wall hiding a room normally used by ad executives monitoring focus groups.

Today the room is occupied by Bobby Bloom, an ex DGSE agent for the French security service. Bloom is a short, balding, spark plug of a man with a neatly trimmed graying beard, fashionably dressed in a black cashmere turtleneck and grey custom-made Savile Row suit. Standing beside Bloom is Paulie St. Clair, an LA lawyer with a gambling problem.

St. Clair enters the casting room through a side door. He's a handsome, well-dressed man in his middle thirties wearing a dark business suit and carrying a stack of resumes. He walks up and down the line of women, checking out each applicant. There is an air of tension in the room; each potential hopeful has answered the same casting call:

Beautiful Redhead Needed
Beautiful, redheaded, figure model or actress needed for an exciting live performance to last for several months. No experience needed. Non-Union, Substantial fee, with potential bonus, international travel required.

Paulie: "Good afternoon ladies, thank you for coming today."

Redhead No 2: "How much does this thing pay? I don't want to waste my time if this is one of those low rent deals?"

Redhead No. 4: "This isn't one of those porn things is it?"

Redhead No. 5: "Yeah, do I have to take off my clothes?"

Paulie: "No, this isn't one of those *porn things* but like the casting call specified, figure model experience is an asset. If nudity makes you uncomfortable I suggest you leave, as you would be wasting your time."

Redhead No. 4 and 5 get up and head for the door.

Paulie looks at Redhead No. 2: "To answer your question, the job pays $1,000 US a week for a minimum of five weeks with the option of an extension at the same pay rate. All expenses paid."

The two women halfway out the door, stop, turn around, and retake their seats. Paulie walks over to Redhead No. 1 who is sitting with her legs crossed.

Paulie looks up from a handful of resumes: "You're Lilly?"

Redhead No. 1: "All day... And all night..."

Paulie: "Your hair... is that that a dye job, or is it natural?" She uncrosses her legs...

Redhead No. 1: "All natural honey... check for yourself if you don't believe me."

Paulie walks down the line of seated woman until he stops at Helen. He shuffles through the resumes until he finds the one he's looking for.

Paulie: "Helen Roth? That's your real name?"

Helen: "Yes sir."

Paulie looks at a single sheet of paper with a headshot stapled to the back. "Says here… you're Jewish, born in Israel, orphaned when you where a baby."

Helen: "My parents were killed in a bomb attack."

Paulie: "Were you raised by relatives?"

Helen: "No sir… no relatives. If I ever had any they were killed by the Nazis. I spent the first sixteen years of my life in an orphanage in Tel Aviv."

Paulie: "A pretty girl like you… hard to believe you didn't melt a few hearts." The other women are getting restless and irritated by the attention Helen is receiving.

Helen: "I didn't always look like this. Just an awkward redhead rag-a-muffin…"

Paulie smiles: "So what happened?"

Helen: "I grew-up, got tits, sculpted my body so I could do figure modeling to pay my way through art school, then moved to Toronto."

Paulie: "So tell me Helen… are you tough… tough enough to stand a little heat?"

Helen: "I was in the Israeli army… what do you think?"

Someone knocks twice on the two-way mirror from the other side. Paulie turns and gives the five other women a final look.

Paulie: "Okay… you five can leave, if we're interested we'll get in touch for a call back." Paulie looks back at Helen. "Helen, you stay." The five other women file out of the room disappointed.

THE KING

An old, abandoned warehouse in the newly redeveloped Arts District, east of Little Tokyo and west of the LA River.

The area seemed to transform itself overnight into a hotbed for creative media companies serving Southern California's insatiable appetite for movie and television content.

For Benson Yeung the building is an investment; for King Yeung, his youngest son, it is an opportunity to prove his worth. King Yeung is rich, privileged, and arrogant, not surprising for someone named King. Then again, you'd expect nothing less from the number two son of Benson Yeung, the Dragon Head of the *Hong Mian,* the most powerful crime organization in Los Angeles.

King has a permanent chip on his shoulder, constantly trying to prove himself to his father and older brother Henry, the designated heir apparent.

Where Henry is articulate, polite, and thoughtful, King is shallow, compulsive, and cruel. While Henry dresses conservatively in expensive custom-made suits from the Three Kings tailor shop, King dresses in the latest flashy styles right out of *Hercules*, a Spanish men's fashion magazine that features the cutting-edge of ostentatious peacockery. Bright yellow sports jackets over black silk shirts and skin tight black trousers, tucked into leather boots that lace almost up to his calf were not an unusual King wardrobe ensemble.

King pulls up to the rundown warehouse in his bright red Tesla Roadster. Despite the area's newfound hipster status, no one in his or her right mind would come within ten miles of the warehouse driving an exotic luxury sports car. But he is Benson Yeung's little boy; and anyone who even looked sideways at the red dream machine would find themselves missing several body parts. If you didn't already know who drove the red beast, the *Guan Yu* sticker on the windshield signaled anyone with half a brain to steer clear.

King pulls the cloth rope closing the huge metal door on the antique freight elevator. He presses the number three-button that sends him on a short ride to the top floor. It's the only floor in the building that contained anything other than rusty old bookbinding equipment, left abandoned by the previous owner: a printing company whose owner could not come up with the interest on an ill-advised loan from the senior Yeung, a mistake that cost him the building and a finger on his right hand. The door to the freight elevator opens just in time for King to see the old man sticking his phone in his pocket.

King: "I thought I told you no phone calls."

Walter: "It was nothing... just a wrong number."

King reaches into the old man's pocket and pulls out the phone. "NO FUCKING PHONES! Do you understand?"

Walter: "No phones, I got it."

King takes the phone and flings it across the room. The phone bangs into a sandblasted brick wall smashing into a dozen pieces, landing at the foot of an easel holding a blank 30x40 inch canvas.

King: "Now you understand, no fucking phones!"

The room is well lit, one side contains six easels all holding blank canvases of varying sizes along with several tables overflowing with brushes, paints, and boxes of gold leaf. There's also a drafting table holding a stack of buff colored Antique Whatman art papers.

On the other side of the warehouse floor is what looks like a movie set. The fake room is made of false walls called flats. The room is an exact replica of Gustav Klimt's studio, including a large window running along one side, covered by translucent drapes. In the middle of the room is a wooden drawing easel and beside it, a well-used box of paints resting on a wooden block. The room features a bed and a platform where Klimt's models posed, displaying their most voluptuous assets.

Movie lights are set up so that simulated sunlight can flood into the room. Two other rooms, a bedroom, and a sitting room, are also replicated from large photographs taped to the sandblasted wall.

Antique cameras are positioned to take photographs of the newly hired Helen Roth posing in period costume as Hilde Roth; creating the visual evidence needed to verify the artwork's provenance.

King: "Is everything ready?"

Walter: "Bring me the right girl and I'll give you what you need."

King: "You better old man. This little setup is costing a fortune. Why we needed to replicate all this old shit, I'll never know."

Walter: "Mr. Yeung, each painting could potentially be worth tens of millions, depending on how many you actually release. If you want this plan to work, you have to spend the time and money to get all the pieces in place."

King: "Yeah, yeah... I get it. There are just too many people involved; too many opportunities for rats. But that's not something you have to worry about. I'll look after that end of things."

Walter didn't like the sound of that, but he was in far too deep to get out now, King was not someone you crossed. The young Chinese mobster reaches into his pocket and pulls out his mobile phone to call Mo Fields, master tailor, owner of The Three Kings Tailor Shop, and professional hit man with Blue Lantern status.

King: "Hello Mo... it's King, I need a couple of suits *taken out*, understand. Yeah that's right, they're making me uncomfortable. Sure, sure... the old man knows all about it. I'll be in later today. Okay sure, see you later."

THE *SHAGUA*

The Green Dragon Restaurant, Benson Yeung's private office. Yeung is sitting at his desk looking over several accounting ledgers. The office is decorated in black lacquer Shanghai Art Déco furniture with red silk cushions on the chairs. On the walls are a series of original Zhang Yuan flower paintings. On the desk facing anyone who enters is an eight-inch high statue of *Guan Yu*, the patron warrior saint of the *Hong Mian*, of which, Benson Yeung is the Dragon Head. Resting on the floor leaning up against the desk is Yeung's black ebony cane with a gold Dragon Head handle signifying his position as triad leader. His son, Henry, enters holding his phone.

Henry: "Pop, I've got Mo on the line. He says King called him this morning, and he wants a couple of suits *taken out.*"

Benson: "Does he know the details?"

Henry: "A couple of set decoration guys that work for Arnie Bernardo."

Benson: "*Shagua!* Your brother is a fool." He motions for Henry to hand him the phone. "Hello Mo... It's Benson. Thank you for calling. No, no don't worry about it; it was the right thing to do. The boy is going to give me an ulcer. Those suits must be making him uncomfortable, and that makes me very nervous.

Take'em out but I don't want to see any seams, understand. The mending has to be invisible. No, no, I won't tell King you called. I'll have Henry drop off a little extra something... a bonus for your discretion.

Oh, and tell your little princess, I have a new *Guan Yu* for her to replace the one she gave the cop... Yes, she's a smart little girl, but be careful my friend, girls can be expensive, and the prettier they are, the more expensive they can be. *[laugh]* Yes, yes, I know how much you charge for a suit. "

THE TAP

Across the road from the Green Dragon, in a dimly lit room above a Chinese laundry, Detective Velma Dime listens intently to the wiretap. Her partner Joe Grist comes out of the bathroom, sits down beside her, and slips on the headphones.

The room is a shabby renter dominated by a saggy bed, and decorated with cheap Chinese reproductions, probably produced for eight bucks apiece in Dafen, China, the home of crappy mass-produced paintings. The room is littered with video and audio surveillance equipment, used paper coffee cups, and the remains of three days worth of cholesterol-infused, fast food.

Dime: "What are the chances they're actually talking about suits?"

Grist: "About the same as me becoming the next Queen of England."

Dime: "Yeah, but who are they talking about? Two suits sounds like they're important."

Grist: "I don't know, it sounds to me like they're just trying to cleanup another of little brother's big messes."

Dime: "Maybe we got the wrong phone tapped."

Grist: "We'll never get a warrant for King's phone. Not with what we got so far."

There's a knock on the door. Grist gets up to answer. He opens it and fellow Detective Alvarez enters.

Grist: "Geez, it's about time Alvarez, what did you do, go sightseeing in Compton again..."

Alvarez: "I just wanted to give you two lovebirds enough time to remake the bed."

Dime: "Thin ice Alvarez, you're on very thin ice."

Alvarez: "Joe… your girl hasn't improved in the sense of humor department."

Grist: "Knock it off Al. You don't want to go there."

Alvarez: "Sorry Velma, I didn't mean anything. I was just kidding."

Dime: "Forget it…"

Alvarez: "So… anything exciting happen or have we got forty-eight hours of Egg Foo Yung orders?"

Grist: "Yeah we got something… somebody's going to die, we just don't know who, where, when, or why?"

Alvarez: "Great… I see you guys got a real handle on things."

Grist: "Velma, call the Captain and tell him we need a tail on Mo Fields."

Alvarez: "That tricky bastard… I don't think we'll ever catch him. He's too smart."

Grist: "Makes a hell-of-a suit, that's for damn sure."

Alvarez" "Yeah, you're the only cop I know that can afford his stuff."

Dime: "Joe… Tell him how you made all your money."

Grist: "I keep telling you, Alvarez, it's easy... buy low and sell high."

Alvarez: "Yeah, get the hell outta here so I can get some sleep..." Alvarez starts rummaging through a large size pizza box.

Alvarez: "Geez... you guys could have at least left me one slice." Alvarez turns. Grist and Dime have already left the room.

THE NEWS CONFERENCE

The Beverly Wilshire Hotel, conference room.

Paulie St. Clair is standing at a podium off to the side of a sliding divider wall that cuts the room in half. Hung on the wall are a series of what appears to be six Gustav Klimt drawings. Each drawing is of the same naked redheaded woman erotically sprawled across a bed. The room is filled with reporters shouting out questions to Paulie, who remains silent. The photographers are all pushing and shoving in order to get the best shot.

At the back of the room is an odd group of three people sitting patiently, waiting for things to begin. The fat man is Cyrus Green, a smuggler, thief, and conman who specializes in lost historical artifacts. The eccentric little man with the bug-eyes and oversized white silk puff hankie is Zoltan Monaco, a supposed Professor of Art History, although no one has ever found any record of him graduating from anything other than a Budapest reform school. And finally, there's the lovely porcelain Chinese doll, Sally Yang, looking delightfully like someone who just stepped off the pages of *Glam*, a trendy Japanese fashion magazine.

Paulie: "Good afternoon ladies and gentlemen, I think you're in for a very special treat. Now if everyone can please take their seats, we'll begin."

The reporters all start scrambling for the best seats while the photographers sit, crouch, or kneel in front, a few still trying to get a good shot.

Reporter 1: "Are they real?"

Reporter 2: "Where did they come from?"

Paulie: "Gentlemen… all in good time, now please settle down."

Reporter 3: "Were they recovered from the Nazis?"

Paulie ignores all the questions. "I am going to make a statement and introduce you to the owner of these works of art. After the statement is read, you will each have two minutes with the owner to ask questions or take photographs.

As you have already guessed, these are original Gustav Klimt drawings of Hilde Roth, the famous redheaded Bohemian model that is seen in many of Klimt's finest masterpieces including, *Lady With Hat and Boa, Danae* and *Goldfish.*"

Reporter 1: "How much are they worth?"

Paulie continues to ignore the questions. "Although Klimt never married, he did father a number of children by various models that more or less lived at his studio."

Watching with great interest from a window in a projection room high above the conference hall are King Yeung and master forger Walter Deloote.

Paulie: "As art historians know, many of Klimt's patrons and models were Jewish, resulting in many of his paintings being confiscated and destroyed by the Nazis.

Although the names of the patrons have been preserved, almost all the models have been lost to history, mainly due to his long-time friend and perhaps lover, Emile Floje, destroying all Klimt's correspondence upon his death.

However... the name of one of these muses, the most important, has survived, Hilde Roth. It is clear that Klimt favored Roth in many ways leaving her with a stash of artwork that she was smart enough to hold on to, and to pass on to her granddaughter.

Each of you will receive a dossier with the Roth family history, photographs of Roth and Klimt standing beside several never before seen masterpieces with Roth as model.

None of what you see, and are about to see, is for sale.

And now ladies and gentlemen, may I present to you, Helen Roth, the Great-Great Granddaughter of Hilde Roth."

As he speaks the wall containing the Klimt drawings slides open to reveal the beautiful, thirty-year old Helen Roth standing in front of three large canvases. Each painting features what appears to be a beautiful semi-nude Hilde Roth draped in a brightly colored gold leaf mosaic robe lounging on a bed, surrounded by her shock of red hair. The woman standing in front of the paintings is a dead ringer for the woman in the pictures. In fact the model for the paintings was Helen Roth.

A collective gasp of awe bursts from the audience. After a moment of silence, the audience explodes in a spontaneous chorus of applause.

In the projection room high above the conference hall, King Yeung turns to his master forger, grabs him by the shoulders, looks right into his eyes, and kisses him on the forehead.

King: "You did it old man. You're a fucking genius."

Walter sighs with relief.

King: "Did you destroy the other three canvases like I told you?"

Walter takes out his phone, does a quick search, and hands it to King. He looks down at a video of Walter tossing one of the three duplicate forgeries into a fire of what appears to be already burning canvases. King smiles; he's extremely pleased with himself, and how clever he thinks he is.

King: "Well done… maybe next time we'll try somebody hard." [*laughs*]

IT'S ALL ABOUT THE WHY

Detective Squad Room

Detectives Grist and Dime are sitting at their desks working on reports from their recent Green Dragon wiretap. Detective Alvarez comes in carrying the morning edition of the LA Times.

Dime: "Working half-days Alvarez?" She taps her watch, like an irritated schoolteacher scolding a student for arriving late. Alvarez ignores the taunt and tosses the newspaper on Grist's desk.

Alvarez: "Get a load of this."

Grist looks down at the headline. "Son-of-a-bitch!"

He tosses the paper across his desk to Dime who occupies the desk facing him. She looks down shaking her head as she reads the headline out loud. *"'Set Decoration Warehouse Burns, Two Men Die In The Blaze'* I guess now we know the who and the when."

Grist: "I'm more interested in the why."

Dime: "Son-of-a-bitch!"

Alvarez: "You two are even starting to talk alike… get a room already."

Even though Dime was in an ongoing relationship with ex French DGSE spook, Bobby Bloom, it was pretty obvious to anyone who knew them, that Grist and Dime were more *Mulder and Scully,* than *Holmes and Watson.*

Dime: "Just remember wiseass, we both carry guns."

THE KING'S CON

The basement conservation room of The Los Angeles Gallery of Figurative Art; on a desk in the corner is a copy of the morning newspaper with the headline:

LOST KLIMT MASTERPIECE
DONATED TO LA ART GALLERY,
Klimt Relative Donates New Found Art Treasures
Professor Walter Deloote To Verify Authenticity

The room is filled with all the artwork and photographs donated to the art gallery by Helen Roth. Walter Deloote is carefully examining the phony Klimt he himself painted.

As the son of a major museum patron, King Yeung, offered to donate the services of Walter Deloote, a retired Professor of Art History, and the leading authority on the Symbolism Art Movement and in particular, the works of Gustav Klimt.

King Yeung is taking advantage of his father's long-time patronage of the art gallery. In addition to substantial cash donations, Benson Yeung has donated a number of valuable pieces from his own collection.

The art gallery has no problem taking the mobster's money or artifacts. Yeung inherently understands the value of good public relations, not to mention the substantial tax right off.

In order to gain credibility, King arranged that Helen Roth donate one of the paintings, the six drawings, and all the phony historical photographic evidence to the museum. In return, the museum was obligated to set up a permanent display under the banner of the Helen Roth Collection. The museum was more than happy to accept the arrangement once the authenticity of the work was verified.

King knew the value and credibility of the remaining two paintings would be enhanced if the prestigious art gallery accepted the donations and setup a permanent collection.

By having the canvases authenticated by an acknowledged expert, King hoped to create a more intense demand, and perhaps even a bidding war, despite the fact it was announced they were not for sale. What King didn't know was that Helen Roth's real name was Helen Deloote, the granddaughter of Walter, the man responsible for forging everything including Helen's false identity.

THE FINDER'S FEE

Office of Paulie St. Clair

The oversized conman, Cyrus Green, is sitting in Paulie St. Clair's office along with his associates: the bizarre pseudo Professor, Zoltan Monaco, and the beautiful but deadly Sally Yang, a delicate creature with a heart of ice.

Green is making a pitch for St. Clair to help them acquire the remaining two Klimts for an Austrian industrialist, whose family collection contains several masterpieces stolen by the Nazis, and never recovered.

Whether Green's story is real or some elaborate fairytale remains to be seen. What Paulie does know is that nothing these three con artists say can be taken at face value. Green appears to be the spokesperson for the three.

Green: "Sir... I hope I can address you in the diminutive as Paulie... I believe such informal fashion is appropriate due to the nature of the arrangement we are proposing; an arrangement that in fact will make for a financially rewarding friendship."

Paulie: "Cut the shit Green, what do you want?"

Monaco: "How dare you sir, address my colleague in such a crude fashion?"

Paulie: "Shut the fuck up."

St. Clair turns to Green "Why don't you tell your creepy little pal to stuff that big puff hankie in his mouth, before I shove it up his ass?"
Green chuckles grabbing his enormous belly as it heaves up and down to the rhythm of his laughter.

Paulie: "You think I don't know who you three con artists are? I'm surprised you got the nerve to show your faces in LA, especially with a scheme that involves the Yeungs."

The same group of con artists were involved in *The Red Emperor* disaster that ended with the death of Peter Pretty Boy Chen, and the wounding of Mo Fields and Henry Yeung by the fourth member of the group, Wilbur Krook.

Yang: "Now let's not be too hasty Mr. St. Clair, we have a financially beneficial offer to propose. From what I understand your particular hobbies could always use an infusion of funds."

Green: "Yes, yes my dear... well put. Plain talk is what we need, and plain talk will benefit us all."

Paulie: "You got five minutes to put some money on the table."

Green: "As you wish... plain talk it is. Our client wants Roth's Klimts, and he's willing to offer you a finder's fee to make it happen."

Paulie: "Listen carefully... King Yeung is behind this whole operation. Do you think he's going to deal with you three clowns after your friend, Krook, almost killed his brother? How is Wilbur anyway? Beat up any little old ladies lately? I noticed he didn't emerge from under his rock to attend our little party."

Green: "Ah yes, poor Wilbur, his absence is an unfortunate by-product of that whole unfortunate escapade; but I assure you, our friend is alive and well."

Paulie: "Yeah… I'm sorry to hear that. Everybody wants to lay their hands on those paintings. They could fetch tens of millions at auction, but they're not for sale."

Yang: "We're authorized to offer you a million dollars if you can change Yeung's mind."

Paulie: "Roth owns the paintings not Yeung, but he is acting as her advisor."

Monaco: "Perhaps he's more than her advisor… perhaps they are lovers?"

Paulie" "I thought I told you to shut the fuck up? You creep me out." Monaco starts to object, but Green puts a hand on his shoulder to settle him down.

Yang: "I believe King Yeung is more motivated by hard cash than the ephemeral quality of female companionship."

Paulie: "So we're talking cash?"

Green: "Yes, yes, cash it is, lovely green *lucre* in the amount of forty million dollars, plus one million for your trouble, payable on delivery in San Francisco."

Paulie: "A million… cash? I can't make any promises but I'll see what I can do." The three con artists get up and file out of Paulie's office.

THE CALL

Office of Paulie St. Clair

As soon as Green, Monaco, and Yang leave, Paulie picks up the phone and calls Yeung.

Paulie: "King… it's Paulie.

King: "Yeah… what's up?"

Paulie: "We got a bite. Green and his band of kooks got a buyer and they're offering forty million for the pair."

King: "Green? That guy's got more nerve than Jesse James. Was that punk Krook there… my brother would pay half a million to put him on a slab."

Paulie: "Na… he didn't show, just Green, the phony professor, and your old hostess, Yang."

King: "Yeah… she can join Krook on an adjoining slab."

Paulie: "We're talking forty million. Isn't that the name of the game?"

King: "Sure, sure, if they actually got the dough."

Pailie: "Said they got an Austrian industrialist as the buyer."

King: "And how much did they offer us as a finder's fee?"

Paulie knew better than to mess with King. "A million."

King: "Pocket-change… the cheap bastards."

Paulie: "They'll pay cash on delivery in San Francisco."

King: "Why San Francisco?"

Paulie: "That's where the moneyman is?"

King: "Okay... Make the arrangement. You and Roth can drive the paintings up and make the exchange. Fields and I will follow just to make sure the money doesn't get lost on the way back."

Paulie: "Okay, I'll let you know when." Paulie hangs up.

THE ROAD TRIP

Pacific Coast Highway

Paulie and Helen are driving up the Pacific Coast Highway with the two fake Klimts in the backseat of Paulie's Mercedes. Following several cars behind is Mo Fields and King Yeung.

The Pacific Coast Highway is a beautiful scenic two-lane coastal roadway that runs along the Pacific Ocean. The highway twists and turns like a snake around rocky hilltop ranges on one side and shear vertical drop-offs into the Pacific on the other.

The route is not for the reckless or anyone in a hurry; passing is literally suicidal. At the apex of many of the snake-like humps in the road are viewing areas where people can stop and enjoy the scenery; and for those afraid of heights, it's a chance to catch their breath and settle their nerves.

Fields: "Don't look now but a grey sedan has been tailing us for about an hour."

King looks in the side-view mirror. "We don't own the highway. It could be anyone, besides once you're on this road there's no place else to go."

Fields: "If you say so…"

Paulie and Helen drive quietly listening to music on the car radio. As they come up alongside one of the viewing areas, a black Ford van pulls out hitting them in the rear passenger side fender. The Mercedes does a three-sixty, forcing them into the rocky mountain cliff. The car bounces off the rocks; then ricochets back across the highway.

Paulie and Helen are tossed around like rag dolls, bouncing from one hard surface to another. The Ford careens off the Mercedes and smashes into the mountainside coming to rest in the middle of the highway.

At the same moment, the grey sedan with Monaco driving, darts out into the oncoming lane as if to pass Fields and King, but instead, pulls alongside in an effort to force them into the Pacific. Fields rams the side of the sedan, and the two cars continue bumping and smashing into each other as they barrel down the highway.

Krook, who's driving the black Ford is dazed; he puts the van into what he thinks is park, but the accident has damaged the transmission, and the gearbox is resting precariously between park and reverse.

Out of the corner of Krook's eye, he sees Fields and Monaco battling it out in a deadly game of bumper cars. He scrambles out of the van just in time to see Monaco being forced up the side of the mountain missing the van by inches. The sedan flips over, landing upside-down.

Fields slams on the breaks while violently turning right, forcing the car to spin one hundred and eighty degrees so its rear-end hits the van sitting in the middle of the road. The scene is a total disaster.

Monaco is out cold in the upside-down sedan. Helen is unconscious trapped in the Mercedes, and Paulie is lying at the side of the road holding his head. King is conscious but dazed. Krook has managed to extract the two paintings from the Mercedes and is carrying them to the Ford. Krook manages to get the paintings into the back of the van. He stumbles his way to the driver's side and gets in.

He tries to start the Ford, but it just groans in agony; he tries again, and this time it works. The van's damaged door didn't close properly, so Krook slams it hard, unknowingly nudging the transmission from false park into reverse.

He looks up to see Mo Fields standing right in front of the Ford with his Glock aimed directly at his head.

Krook guns the engine to run-over Fields, but instead of lurching forward, the Ford takes off backwards racing over the cliff before Krook realizes what is happening.

Fields walks to the Mercedes and helps Helen out. As Helen, Paulie, and King watch, Fields uses the Mercedes to slowly push the grey sedan over the side of the cliff with a moaning Monaco still in it.

King: "The fucking paintings! Where are they?"

Fields just points out into the middle of the Pacific Ocean.

THE REPERCUSSION

Benson Yeung's office

Benson is sitting at his desk reading the morning edition of the LA Times. His oldest son Henry is standing off to the side waiting arms folded. His youngest son, King, is sitting across from his father tapping his toe anxiously. The old man stops reading, puts the paper down, and gives his youngest son a hard stare.

Benson: "I don't see that any money was transferred into our account."

King: "We were hijacked Pop, that son-of-a-bitch Green set us up. He had Krook and Monaco waiting for us."

Benson: "Fields already told me the details. What I want to know is, are you completely stupid?"

Henry: "How much did this little caper of yours cost us?"

Benson looks at Henry as if to say shut the fuck up, I'll handle this. Henry shuts up.

King: "Not that much Pop… the whole deal was a hundred thousand… maybe a hundred and fifty."

Henry: "Jesus fucking Christ, a hundred and fifty thousand, pissed away on some stupid…"

Benson fires a warning look at his eldest son, who immediately quiets down.

Benson: "What about the redhead and the artist?"

King: "They took off. The hijacking really scared them. As soon as they got back, they packed-up and ran… didn't even ask for their last pay checks."

Benson: "Are they going to be a problem?"

King: "No way Pop, they couldn't get out of LA fast enough."

Benson: "What about the paintings and the bodies?"

King: "The ocean just swallowed them lock, stock, and paintings. I'm sorry Pop. They're just gone."

Benson: "It's too bad you burned the other paintings; we could have at least salvaged something out of this mess. Let this be a lesson. Always have a Plan B."

King: "You want me to track down the girl and the artist?"

Benson: "Just leave it be. I doubt they'll be a problem. Let's not make this any worse than it already is."

King: "Sure Pop, whatever you say…"

Benson: "I think you should take a vacation, a nice long vacation. And don't come back till you get your head out of your ass. Now get the hell out of here before I lose my temper."

King gets up and leaves. Henry looks at his father and just shakes his head. "It's a damn good thing Mo was there to clean up his mess."

Benson: "Send him over a little extra bonus. He's a valuable asset. I don't know how two sons can be so different?" The old man picks up his newspaper and starts to read it again.

EPILOGUE
THE ART OF THE GRIFT
Always Have A Plan B

Windsor Arms Hotel, Yorkville District, Toronto

Bobby Bloom sits in a black leather club chair sipping a brandy in a suite at the fashionable Windsor Arms Hotel; a place favored by celebrities and politicians for its service and discretion. Leaning up against the wall are two large black cases holding the second copies of the forged Klimt canvases, the ones that were supposed to be burned.

FLASHBACK: Walter burning two blank canvases while Helen videos him as he tosses the third duplicate Klimt into the fire. Walter turns to Helen just as she finishes videoing...

Walter: "Always have a Plan B my dear; you never know how these things will play out."

There's a knock on the door. Bloom gets up, goes to the door and opens it. A tall dour man with a moustache and thinning black hair nods silently. Bloom can almost hear the clicking of his heels as he imagines his guest in a black SS uniform.

Christoph Fuchs is an Austrian art dealer who represents one of his countries wealthiest industrial magnates, a man who also happens to be a collector of turn-of-the-century Austrian artists like Gustav Klimt and Egon Schiele.

The client is a man with too much money and not enough scruples to worry about small details like provenance, even if the *objet d'arte* is a stolen Nazi painting. As a French Jew, Bobby Bloom has no problem taking this man's money for a couple of relatively worthless forgeries.

Fuchs: "Herr Bloom…"

Bloom: "Herr Fuchs…"

Fuchs enters the room and glances over at the two large black cases. Bloom nods and waves a hand extending an offer for Fuchs to take a look. Fuchs moves to the cases and one by one removes the canvases and leans them up against the bed. He crouches down on one knee and inspects them.

Fuchs: "Beautiful… wonderful workmanship… the man was a genius, an Austrian hero. My client will be pleased."

Bloom hands Fuchs a piece of paper with two numbered accounts written in pencil. He points to the laptop on the desk and motions for Fuchs to sit.

Bloom: "As agreed then, one point five million dollars into the first account, my fee; and forty million into the second account as payment for the paintings."

Fuchs nods his head, and this time Bloom swears he hears the Austrian click his heels together. Fuchs makes the entries into the computer, with Bloom carefully observing over his shoulder. With the business part of the transaction done, Fuchs places the canvases back into their cases and leaves.

Bloom goes to the door that connects his room to the adjoining suite; he knocks on the door; it opens. A smiling Helen Deloote grabs Bloom and gives him a big hug and kiss on the cheek. Helen's grandfather Walter pops the cork on a $300 bottle of Cristal Brut Champagne. He pours each of them a glass.

Helen: "Make sure Paulie gets his cut. We don't want any problems."

Bloom: "I'll look after him out of my share, but knowing him, I doubt his half a million will last long."

Walter: "I believe it's time to toast our success… and my retirement."

THE END

The Incident Report

If It's Not Reported, It Didn't Happen

JERRY BADER

THE INCIDENT

Edwards Air Force Base, Debriefing Room

Major Willard White sits patiently in a dimly lit room on an uncomfortable grey metal chair. The only other furniture in the room is a metal table and one other matching chair. A pitcher of water and a single glass sit on the table. The room is dark with one flickering overhead florescent that illuminates the table. The only other light in the room is from the barely visible red record light on the camera mounted in the upper corner of the room.

White has been waiting thirty minutes, and he's grown increasingly agitated. He reaches for the pitcher, pours a glass of water, and drinks. The door opens and two men enter. The Major squints hard to make out the two men, but neither is familiar. The man holding a file folder stuffed with papers wears the uniform of a Brigadier General; the other is in civilian clothes. White rises to salute.

General: "At ease Major."

The General sits down across the table from White while the civilian stands off to the side. The General opens the file folder marked "Top Secret" in red and slides a piece of paper across the table.

General: "I think there's been a clerical mistake with your report." There is no mistake. White knows exactly what the General is referring to, and he almost expected it.

White: "That's what happened Sir."

General: "I really don't give a shit what you think happened. You're wrong, understand. You made a mistake. You handed in a draft before you had a chance to think about it."

White: "General… I've been doing this for a long time. I know what I saw. There's evidence, radar evidence, photographic evidence, and cockpit recordings. It's not something that can just disappear."

General: "That's where you're wrong son, anything can disappear… including people that file misleading, erroneous reports." The General doesn't even bother to try to couch the threats in some kind of semantic cloud.

General: "Do it over. And this time, do it properly, or there will be consequences. You don't want something like this to screw-up your life. You've had a damn fine career. Don't fuck it up."

The General gets up and leaves the room, but the civilian remains. With the General gone, the civilian sits down across from the Major. He flashes his NSA credentials: *John Smith, Senior Specialist.* He takes a photograph out of the folder the General left on the table.

Smith: "You know this woman." The photograph is of a very attractive woman who happens to be White's fiancée.

White: "You know damn well, I know her."

Smith: "An actress… must be nice. I'm sure you wouldn't want anything bad to happen to a nice looking woman like that."

White: "Now wait just a goddamn minute! She's got nothing to do with this. She's a civilian, and I haven't even spoken to her since I landed."

Smith: "Well I'm glad to hear that. Maybe you don't care about your pension, or what you'll be able to do after you retire… and you are retiring, but it would be a shame to see someone so young run into trouble… be smart. Let this go. If you're worried about the radar and other stuff… don't! Let us worry about that. You just write a nice innocuous report, retire, have babies, and enjoy life."

Smith puts the photograph back in the file folder and pushes the report closer to White. He taps the report several times with his finger. "We all follow orders Major... be a good boy and do what you're told."

He gets up and leaves. White looks at the report and the red light on the camera in the top corner of the room opposite where he's sitting. He rips the report in half and stuffs the pieces in his pocket. Back at his desk he notices a thick manila envelope. He opens it to find all the papers needed to file for retirement. Everything is already filled in; all he has to do is sign it, but he doesn't. He takes his cell phone out of his desk drawer and calls Grace, his fiancée.

White: "Grace... I'm just leaving the office now. I should be home in a couple of hours." He hangs up and heads out.

FLASHBACK: Forty-five minutes earlier

Smith enters the Debriefing Room carrying a pitcher of water and a single glass. It's dark with only a sliver of light coming into the room from the open door. There are two switches on the wall; he flips the first one, but nothing appears to happen, so he tries the second. The florescent light that hangs over the table blinks sporadically for a few seconds before it finally settles into an irritating flickering hum. He pushes the door closed with his foot so no one can see in.

Smith: "Fucking figures... just like the military, even the lights only half work." He takes a small envelope out of his jacket pocket and removes several digoxin tablets. He drops the tablets into the pitcher and stirs the water with a tongue depressor until the pills dissolve. He wraps the wooden stick in a dry tissue and sticks it in his jacket pocket.

THE DECISION

UPS Store, Studio City, California

Two hours later, White pulls into a parking spot in front of a UPS Store about a half a mile from Grace's Studio City apartment. Something is wrong: he's agitated, dizzy, and beads of sweat are running down his back despite having the air conditioning cranked up. The politics were making him sick to his stomach. As a fighter pilot, and more recently a test pilot, he was used to stress, but this was different, very different.

White: "Fuck it. Maybe it is time to retire."

He gets out of his car and goes into the UPS Store. He takes the torn report out of his pocket and stuffs it into an envelope. He carefully prints a name and address on the envelope, and hands it to the sales clerk along with a ten-dollar bill. He collects his change and leaves for Grace's.

He never makes it.

BAD NEWS

Grace Edwards' Studio City apartment.

Grace and White live in a three-bedroom Bluffside Drive apartment about a block from Ventura Blvd, a short drive to most of the major studios including Bernardo Productions. White should have been home an hour-and-half ago. She knows something is wrong. White has been unusually quiet lately, but whatever it was, he wasn't talking. The sound of the main door buzzer startles her. She gets up to answer.

Grace: "Yes… who is it?"

Policeman One: "LAPD, can we come up?"

Grace presses the button to let them into the building. A few minutes later there's a knock on the door. Grace looks out the peephole to see two uniformed police officers. She opens the door to let them in.

Police One: "Are you Grace Edwards?"

Grace: "Yes, what's going on? Has something happened to Will?"

Police One: "I'm afraid we have bad news. He's had a heart attack, and unfortunately he didn't make it."

Grace: "What! What are you talking about? I just spoke to him a couple of hours ago. There must be some mistake…"

Police One: "Major Willard White, USAF. I'm afraid there's no mistake…"

Tears start running down Grace's face. She stares at the two policemen in disbelief. She feels faint and is about to collapse.

The second policeman catches her before she falls and helps her to a couch in the living room off to the side of the vestibule.

Police One: "Get her some water."

The second policeman goes to the kitchen and comes back with a glass of water that he hands to Grace. She takes a sip and places the glass on a coaster on the end table beside the couch.

Police One: "We're deeply sorry Ma'am, but Major White suffered a significant heart attack coming out of the UPS Store on Ventura. He was gone before the paramedics arrived."

Grace: "That can't be… he's too young. He's a test pilot for god's sake… he's as healthy as can be… This has got to be a mistake?"

Police One: "I'm afraid there's no mistake. These things happen."

Grace is stunned. The senior policeman hands her his card, and they leave. She's left alone with her runaway thoughts.

Grace replays the news over in her head. There must be more to this than meets the eye. White hadn't been himself for days, something was bothering him, something was very wrong. This whole thing stinks. She picks up the phone and dials Lonnie Bernardo's number. "Lonnie… it's Grace, Grace Edwards, I've got to see you and Arnie, as soon as possible."

AIN'T NO JOHNNY CASH

Grace Edwards' Studio City apartment, the following day.

The buzzer rings and Grace rushes to press the button to allow Lonnie and Arnie Bernardo into the building. Grace is starring in a new movie being produced by Bernardo Productions. Since she's been hired, she's become very close to Arnie and his wife Lonnie. Arnie is an ex gangster turned movie producer and over the last while his company has become a major player in the industry.

There's a knock on the door. She opens it expecting to see the Bernardos, but instead there's a forty something man wearing aviator sunglasses, a black suit, white shirt, and black tie.

Grace: "Who the hell are you?" He flashes his credentials: "Smith… John Smith, NSA."

Grace: "Very imaginative…"

Smith: "Ma'am?"

Grace: "The name… doesn't anybody in the government have an imagination."

Smith: "I wouldn't know about that, Miss Edwards… you are Grace Edwards aren't you?"

Grace: "Yes, I'm Grace… look I don't know who you are, or what you want, but now is a bad time."

Smith: "I'm here to offer our condolences for the loss of your fiancé, Major White."

Grace: "Thank you, but I am expecting some friends and…"

Smith just brushes past her and walks into the living room.

"This won't take long. I just have a few questions that need answering."

Grace follows the man in black into the living room. She takes a seat on the couch leaving Smith standing in the middle of the room.

Grace: "Okay… ask."

Smith: "Have you noticed anything strange or different about the Major's behavior lately?"

Grace: "I don't know… maybe he's been a little distracted… he's been pretty quiet the last week or so."

Smith: "Did he give you a piece of paper, a kind of draft report by any chance?"

Grace: "No… why would he do that? He doesn't talk to me about his work."

Smith: "You went to hospital last night to identify the body, and pickup his things." It's more of a statement than a question.

Grace: "Yes…"

Smith: "Perhaps he left it in the pocket of his uniform?"

Grace: "There was nothing, just his wallet and some loose change."

Smith: "Do you mind if I look around, I'd really like to find that report?"

Grace: "Yes I mind. I don't have your report. Will never talked to me about any report. And I want you to leave. I have a funeral to plan."

Smith: "You're making a mistake Miss Edwards. You really should co-operate. That report is government property. It never should have left the base, and if you're caught with it, you could be charged with a violation of Homeland Security Laws."

Grace: "Get out! Get out now before I throw you out. How dare you come in here accusing me, or Will? He was a war hero, you asshole. I don't know anything about your fucking report…"

The buzzer rings. Grace gets up, goes to the door to let the Bernardos into the building. When she returns to the living room Smith is rummaging through the desk in the corner of the room.

Grace: "What do you think you're doing? Get the fuck out of here before I call the police."

Smith: "You really don't want to cause trouble. It would be a big mistake. You've already lost your fiancé; you don't want to lose your career… or worse." There's a knock on the door.

Grace: "You better leave!"

Smith heads for the door puts his hand on the door handle, and turns, handing Grace his card. "If you find the report, call, call me right away… and for your own sake, don't read it."

He opens the door to see Lonnie and Arnie Bernardo standing there. He nods and heads down the hall for the elevator. The Bernardos enter the apartment. Lonnie looks at Grace, who is obviously upset.

Lonnie: "Who was that?"

THE BERNARDO MEETING

Grace Edwards Studio City apartment

Grace is close to hysterical: Will's heart attack, seeing the body, and now the asshole from the NSA. The whole thing stinks to high heaven, and she's determined to find out where the smell is coming from. It takes Lonnie and Arnie about fifteen minutes to calm her down.

Grace: "Arnie, you know people, people who can find things out. I know you do, please help me?"

Arnie: "I wish I could, but you know I'm not in that business anymore."

Lonnie: "Maybe Vito and Sid could nose around?"

Arnie: "These guys aren't gangsters. We're talking about the NSA and the Air Force."

Grace: "They're acting like gangsters."

Arnie: "This requires some finesse; subtlety isn't Vito and Sid's strong suit."

Lonnie: "Arnie, please... we've got to do something. This isn't right."

Arnie: "Yeah, something isn't kosher... Will was healthy as a horse." Arnie takes out his cell phone and dials Bobby Bloom's number. Bloom, owns the Montmartre Gallery Bistro, but his real job is fixing sticky situations for Arnie and his friends.

The ex DGSE agent for the French Security Service has the necessary expertise and government connections to find things out that shouldn't be found. If anybody could help, it's Bloom.

Arnie: "Bobby... it's Arnie. Good, good, yeah, Lonnie's great, gorgeous as ever. Listen, can you meet me at the office? I've got a delicate situation that needs your special expertise. Okay my friend... I'll see you there in an hour."

Lonnie: "Bloom?"

Arnie nods to Lonnie and turns to Grace. "I've got somebody who used to travel in those circles. He may be able to find something out. No promises... this is tricky... and I don't know how far we can push it."

Lonnie: "If anybody can find out what really happened, and why that report is so goddamn important, it's Bobby Bloom."

THE LETTER

Bullpen WNGB - World News Gazette Blog

A young female rookie reporter, Ricky Saks, drops a single envelope on Sol Sherman's desk.

Sherman: "What's this?" Sherman still wasn't used to the casual environment of his new Internet employer.

Saks: "This rag *ain't* the *Times*, Sol. You better get used to it, or it'll eat you up inside."

Sol Sherman was a top reporter for the *New York Times*. He covered all the Middle East wars, major international scandals, and just about every significant news event of the last ten years. He was being groomed to be the next Walter Cronkite, the most trusted newsman in the country, but that was before he filed a report that accused an up-and-coming Tea Party candidate of influence peddling.

The party didn't like the way Sherman portrayed their boy in the *Times*, so they feed him a bunch of misinformation.

Sherman corroborated all the stories with party insiders who told him the guy was corrupt, but it was all an elaborate setup aimed at destroying his credibility. All his sources denied ever saying anything bad about the man and Sherman was hung out to dry. He was accused of making it all up to destroy the candidate's career because he didn't like his politics. The fact is, the guy was as crooked as a dog's hind leg, but nobody was willing to back up Sherman. As far as the paper was concerned, it didn't matter he was set-up; what mattered was he fell for it. His career as a big-time newsman was over. All that was left was a staff job at an LA start-up news blog.

Sherman takes his letter opener and slits the envelope open. He takes out two crumpled pieces of paper; one with a USAF logo on the top.

Saks: "Anything interesting?"

Sherman ignores the question. He sees that the two pieces of paper are actually one incident report by a Major Willard White.

Sherman: "You got any tape?"

Saks hands Sherman the tape dispenser from her desk. He tapes the two pieces together and reads carefully.

Saks: "If it's interesting, I want in." She gets up to try to look over Sherman's shoulder.

Sherman: "Sit the fuck down. You don't want any part of this."

Saks: "Asshole! I thought you were a nice guy."

Sherman: "Listen kid, if this is real, this could be trouble... big trouble."

Saks: "Sure, hog it for yourself."

Sherman: "Trust me Ricky, you don't want any part of this."

Saks: "Wake up tough guy, if it's that big, who the hell's going believe it coming from you? You aren't that guy any more... You need me!"

Sherman stops and thinks for a second. "Maybe... I don't know..."

Saks: "Come on Sol, I can help. Give a chance. Maybe we both can come out of this with something better than this dump."

Sherman takes the taped report and places it back in the envelope. He puts it in his desk drawer, but then thinks better of the idea; instead, he puts it in the inside pocket of the jacket hanging on the back of his chair.

Sherman: "Tell you what, let me see if this thing is for real, if it is, we'll work on it together, but you got to follow my lead, understand."

Saks: "Sure, absolutely, you're the boss…"

Sherman: "Not the boss kid, just the guy with ten years experience."

Saks: "Look, I'm sorry about the crack, I know you're a great reporter."

Sherman: "Okay partner, we got a deal, but I have to see if this is legit."

Saks: "Give me something, anything, what's it about."

Sherman: "Not yet… not till I find out a bit more. Anyway, it's better if you don't know."

Saks: "Give me something… anything. Point me in a direction, and I'll show you I can do it."

Sherman sits back in his chair and looks hard at the attractive young woman now perched on the corner of his desk.

Sherman: "Tell you what. Find out everything you can about an air force pilot, Major Willard White, but whatever you do, don't talk to anyone in the military or the government."

Saks: "How the hell am I going to do that?"

Sherman: "You want in or not?"

Saks: "I'm in! No military or government. Got it!"

Sherman: "Just be careful. Don't make me regret I brought you in on this. I wouldn't want to see you get hurt."

Saks: "Well if I didn't know better, I might think you're sweet on me."

Sherman: "You could do worse."

Saks: "I guess I could."

THE DISC

Edwards Air Force Base, Video Surveillance Room

The Video Surveillance Room features a bank of fifteen medium-sized video monitors surrounding two larger monitors all mounted on a semi-circular wall. Facing the monitors is a large semi circular desk with three more monitors.

Sitting in one of the three ergonomically designed black leather chairs in the middle of the desk is Airman Pat Jublonski. The two other chairs are empty.

Jublonski isn't happy about being stuck in the room alone. The two other airmen tasked with overseeing the monitors were reassigned, and he was waiting for their replacements. Like everything else in the military, nothing happens quickly, at least, nothing good.

The door opens and Captain Wilkinson comes in carrying a handful of video surveillance discs. Jublonski jumps up, snaps to attention, and salutes the officer.

Wilkinson: "At ease airman as you were." Wilkinson drops the pile of discs on the desk in front of Jublonski. "These are the debriefing discs from the last few days. Visually scan them to make sure everything's in order then file them where they belong."

Jublonski: "Sir, can it wait till I get some help in here. It's kind of hard looking at all these monitors and checking these discs at the same time."

Wilkinson: "Tell you what Jublonski if you rather be in the Gulf, I can arrange it. So what do you say?"

Jublonski: "No Sir, no problem, check the discs and file them, top priority... SIR!"

Wilkinson turns and leaves.

Jublonski: "More crap to do. Just keep piling on the busy work like it's easy looking at fifteen things at once, all by myself." He catches himself from saying anything else as he realizes that the bastards might even have the video room monitored. He looks at the pile of discs and figures he might as well get started. He picks up the one on top, slips it into the disc player and watches the images spring to life on the large computer screen directly in front of him.

After about two hours of boring interviews, he's only half through the pile. He gets up to stretch, walks around the room in a circle, and stands in front of the monitors with his hands on his hips. He's frustrated and bored. He picks up the next disc on the pile and slams it hard into the player. The screen goes dark with just a sliver of light illuminating one of the debriefing rooms.

Jublonski: "Shit! What now." He goes to pop the disk out to see if he damaged it, but before he does, he sees a florescent light blink several times before it settles into a flickering beam illuminating the metal table and chairs in Debriefing Room Two. He sits down and watches intently. He doesn't see anyone, but he hears an unfamiliar voice.

Voice: "Fucking figures... just like the military, even the lights only half work."

Jublonski is fixed on the screen. He hears the door shut and a man in a black suit walks into the frame holding a pitcher of what appears to be water in one hand, and a glass in the other. Jublonski leans in closer as if it would give him a better view. He's seen this guy around the past few days and rumor has it, he's one of those NSA assholes. He watches the guy take a packet out of his pocket and drop a bunch of pills into the pitcher. He takes a stick out of his pocket and stirs the concoction. He wraps the stick in some kind of tissue, sticks it in his pocket, and exits the frame. He hears the door open and the florescent light is turned off. He hears the door close, and the room goes black.

Jublonski looks at the scrubber bar on the video and sees that there is a lot more on the disc, he sits and watches nothing for about a minute. Then, the light in the room goes on and he hears one of the other airmen usher Major White into the room. He remembers hearing White had a heart attack and died a few days ago. He stops the video and checks the metadata for the video and sure enough, the video was taken the same day White died.

He restarts the video. The Major sits down in the chair opposite the camera. Jublonski watches fixated on the screen for about thirty minutes. White just sits there, getting more and more agitated. Finally he reaches for the spiked pitcher of water, pours a glass, and drinks.

A few seconds later, two men walk in. Their backs are to the camera. He can tell from the star on his shoulder that the man in uniform is a Brigadier General, but he doesn't recognize him. He can't see the other man's face either, but he identifies him as the guy that spiked the pitcher of water. Jublonski watches the rest of the disc as the two men take turns trying to intimidate Major White. He heard rumors that something strange happened on one of the test flights but as soon as you asked anybody about it, they'd clam-up.

Jublonski sits back in the chair and stares at the now black screen. What the hell is he going to do? There's no way in hell this was ever supposed to be videoed. The suit must have thought one of the switches on the wall was a light switch and didn't realize it turned on the surveillance system. That's what prompted the crack about military efficiency.

Jublonski had to protect his ass but how? He reaches under the desk and pulls out a stack of blank discs. He puts a blank in the second disc player connected to the second desk monitor. He presses a few buttons so the video appears on both monitors, hits record, and starts the video again from the beginning.

BOBBY'S BEAT

Montmartre Gallery Bistro

Leon Bailey is busy getting the restaurant ready for the coming evening. Bailey actually runs the restaurant since Bloom is usually too busy solving problem situations for his movie business friends.

Bailey's is more than a *maitre de* and restaurateur, he's Bloom's main operative. In fact most of the restaurant staff have responsibilities beyond mere food service: the restaurant is really a front for Bloom's private security and corporate intelligence business.

Bailey is an impressive man. He's a tall, coffee-colored Jamaican, elegantly dressed in a black custom-made suit, crisp white shirt, and a vertically stripped, black and white silk tie. He speaks with a deep baritone accent.

The Montmartre is *the* spot for Hollywood's elite, an odd assortment of entertainment people, gangsters, and successful arty types. The place is decorated in pulp fiction style paintings and Rennie Mackintosh furniture, a classy mix of art and style that matches Bloom's personality.

Bloom is a short, balding man with a neatly trimmed graying beard. He always can be seen wearing a turtleneck, bespoke Savile Row suit, and a Barak SP21 semi-automatic.

Bloom sits at a table in the corner drinking coffee as he goes over the evening's reservations. Agent Smith enters letting the stained glass door close behind him. Bailey spots him and moves quickly to intercept as he heads for Bloom.

Bailey: "Good afternoon sir, can I help you?"

Smith flashes his NSA badge but Bailey stands his ground.

Smith: "Get out of my way."

Smith steps around Bailey but finds himself confronted by two waiters dressed in white shirts, black silk ties, and black trousers, each carrying rather large kitchen knifes.

Bloom: "It's okay Leon..."

Bailey nods to the two waiters who resume their table setting duties. Bailey heads for the bar while Smith sits down opposite Bloom. "Can't say as I think much of the service in this place."

Bloom: "Well... we do try to keep the riffraff to a minimum."

Bailey arrives at the table, delivering a fresh pot of coffee and a cup for Smith. He pours the coffee and heads back to the bar.

Smith: "Just what the hell do you think you're doing?"

Bloom: "Trying to get ready for this evening's guests."

Smith: "Cut the shit Bloom. Did you think no one would notice you poking around this White business?"

Bloom: "You didn't handle the fiancée very well, did you? You scared the crap out of her. A little finesse and you might have got away with it, but no, that's not your style, is it?"

Smith: "Keep out of it."

Bloom: "You want me out... give something to tell my client. She's pissed. And she's got friends."

Smith pauses, strokes his chin as he thinks... "What do you know about Special Report 13?"

Bloom smiles and shakes his head as if in disbelief. "You got to be kidding?"

Smith: "It's true… fucking photographs, radar… the whole nine yards."

Bloom: "So you killed the guy? He was a war hero for god's sake."

Smith: "He wouldn't play ball, insisting on filing a detailed report."

Bloom: "Our governments have been burying this kind of thing since '47. What's the big deal?"

Smith: "They… or it… or whatever the hell it was, shot up his plane. He's lucky he was able to land it. Experimental job worth a fortune… and he wasn't prepared to shut-up about it."

Bloom: "Yah well I don't blame him. Besides you assholes can't go around killing war heroes because you can't handle a little heat."

Smith: "The report's missing, he didn't hand it in, and the fiancée says, she doesn't have it."

Bloom: "You got a problem all right… but killing the guy, a bit drastic don't you think?"

Smith: "Not my call. I just do what I'm told. So play it smart *mon ami*… you're still a foreigner. If you don't want to find yourself on the next flight back to *Gay Paireé*, you'd better back the hell off."

Bloom: "Okay… I get it. I don't want a problem, but leave the girl alone. She doesn't know anything."

Smith: "It's not just us. It knocked out everybody's satellites for three hours. The Whitehouse phones lit up like that stupid monster Christmas tree they erect every year."

Bloom: "I'll tell them I hit a dead end. The guy just had a heart attack. Shit happens." Bloom takes out his cell phone and punches in Arnie Bernardo's private number. "Arnie… *c'est moi… Oui… oui…* écoutez… I've hit a dead end. This thing is too big. We don't want any trouble. Tell Grace it was a heart attack caused by stress. It happens. *Oui… oui…* I'm sorry too."

Smith nods approval, drains his coffee in one gulp and leaves. Bailey comes over to clear the dirty cup. "You want someone to keep an eye on him?"

Bloom thinks for a moment. "You know what? That's not a bad idea. I'd hate to see anything happen to White's fiancée. The guy knows his business so make sure it's somebody good… and somebody not associated with us.

Bailey nods, then goes to make the arrangement

SAKS AND THE FLYBOY

The Flyboy, a 1950s style diner decorated in Air Force memorabilia and frequented by the enlisted men working at Edwards.

Ricky Saks has been making progress by following leads based on the rumors she's heard from the men at the diner. She's made contact with Airman Pat Jublonski, the tech who's responsible for filing the debriefing videos.

It wasn't hard for an attractive woman like Saks to get a horny airman to start talking. If Sol was going to trust her she had to come up with something and today was the day.

Jublonski is sitting at the table furthest from the door and away from the other men in the diner. He's reading the newspaper. Saks stops at the door to unbutton an extra button on her shirt. She's wearing skin-tight jeans that show-off her figure. She hopes it's enough to get what she wants. She needs Jublonski drooling if she's going to get the evidence. She walks in and every guy with a heartbeat stops eating and stares as she makes her way to Jublonski table. She sits down on the banquette opposite the airman.

Saks: "Do you have it?"

Jublonski can't help but stare.

Saks: "Pat... do you have it?"

Jublonski: "Yah, it's in my pocket."

Saks: "Can I have it, please?"

Jublonski: "I don't know. I could get into deep shit. This is dangerous..."

Saks: "They killed him, Pat. The guy was a fucking Major in the United States Air Force. A war hero! Is that okay with you?"

Jublonski: "Of course not… White was a good guy. He was just doing his job."

A waitress comes over, puts down a cup and saucer in front of Saks and pours some coffee without asking. She takes a pencil from behind her ear and an order pad from her belt.

Waitress: "What can I get you?"

Saks: "Just the coffee… thanks."

Jublonski: "They got great muffins… you should try one."

Saks: "The coffee's fine, I'm watching my figure."

Waitress: "Honey… so is every guy in the place."

Saks: "Just the coffee." The waitress shrugs and leaves. "Look Pat… you're in a position to do something about it. We need that disc!"

Jublonski: "They ever find out I gave you the disc… I'd be the next one with a toe tag."

Saks: "Look… the disc is your best protection. Right now they don't even know they recorded it. It's filed away and forgotten about. They find out there's evidence and you're the only one who's seen it, you sure as hell will end up on a slab. But if the evidence is out in the public, they can't do a damn thing."

Jublonski: "I don't know Ricky. You come in here dressed like that… I'm not an idiot. I know what you want. You're not interested in me. You just want the goddamn disc."

Saks: "You're right Pat, and I'm sorry, but this thing is bigger than you and I..."

Jublonski: "I don't even know why they did it."

Saks: "But you know they did, and it's not right."

Jublonski reaches into his jacket pocket, pulls out the disc and slips it between the pages of the newspaper. He slides the paper across the table. Saks gets up, picks up the paper, and whispers in his ear. "You're doing the right thing."

She kisses him on the cheek and leaves the diner. Saks gets into her car and heads back to the office to check out the disc and tell Sherman what she's got. Saks is excited and doesn't realize how fast she's driving until a State Trooper flashes his headlights in her rear mirror.

Saks: "SHIT!"

Saks tries to apply the brakes to slow down but nothing happens. The State Trooper starts honking his horn but sees Saks is in trouble. He puts on his siren and cars start pulling off the highway. The Trooper pulls up alongside Saks and she yells... "NO BRAKES!"

The cop pulls ahead of Saks cutting in front of her. He gradually slows, allowing Saks' car to bang into his bumper, slowing her down. Gradually they ease the two cars off to the shoulder. Saks sits staring blankly out the car window paralyzed by fear. The Trooper taps on the side window and waits till she rolls it down.

Trooper: "Are you all right, Ma'am?" No answer. "Ma'am, are you okay?"

She nods without turning. The Trooper kneels down under the car and shines s flashlight to inspect the under carriage. He gets up and goes over to Saks who has recovered enough to get out of the car.

Trooper: "Looks like somebody tampered with your brakes. Any idea who that might be?" Saks shakes her head.

PUBLISH AND PERISH

WNGB Boardroom

Saks and Sherman are having an animated discussion after reviewing Major White's Incident Report and surveillance disc.

Sherman: "Jesus Ricky, they tried to kill you. I don't want to see you get hurt. I never should have got you involved. Maybe we should back off."

Saks: "Not a chance... I say we take it to Phil right now."

Sherman reluctantly nods okay, and they head for Phil Tailor's office, the Managing Editor. The door is closed so they knock and enter.

Sherman: "Phil, we've got something..."

Tailor: "Who said you could barge into my office, Can't you see I'm in a meeting?" Sherman and Saks turn their heads and notice Smith sitting in the corner.

Saks: "We'll come back."

Smith: "Ricky Saks?"

Saks: "Yes..."

Smith: "You met with a Pat Jublonski earlier today?"

Saks: "Who?"

Smith gets up and walks toward Saks, but Sherman steps in front of her blocking his way. "Who the hell are you?"

Smith: "Be smart you two, turn over everything you've got and we'll forget you've broken about a dozen laws."

Sherman: "We don't know what you're talking about."

Tailor: "Look; whatever you're working on drop it. You might as well co-operate because whatever it is, it's not getting published here or anyplace else for that matter."

Smith: "I'm doing you guys a favor. You really should pay attention, cause this is something you really don't want to do. Bad things happen to people who make stupid decisions. "

Saks: "Like tampering with my brakes?"

Smith sidesteps Sherman and reaches for the door. "Be smart Miss Saks, you've already had one close call; your friend Jublonski wasn't so lucky."

Saks: "Pat? Why what happened to him?"

Smith: "Oh… it's Pat is it? Thought you never heard of him? It's really too bad though, a young man like that… cut down in the prime of his life."

Saks: "What the hell did you do to him?"

Smith: "Hit by a car. Killed instantly from what I understand."

Smith takes two cards out of his jacket and stuffs one in Sherman's shirt pocket and the other in Saks', lingering just a little too long doing it."

Saks: "Pig!"

Smith: "I want the report and the disc Jublonski gave you. And I want it fast. Don't be stupid. I'll expect to hear from you by the end of the day."

Sherman: "Or what?"

Smith: "Or else, asshole... or else!"

Sherman and Saks go back to their desks.

Saks: "What do we do?"

Sherman: "I already talked to a friend at *The Times* and he says they won't touch it. Everybody's been scared off."

Saks: "What about blogging it ourselves?"

Sherman: "We'll just look like crackpots: conspiracy theory nuts, especially with my history."

An Intern appears at Sherman's desk.

Sherman: "Yah, what's up?"

Intern: "Somebody dropped this off a few minutes ago." He hands Sherman an envelope and leaves. Sherman looks at Saks and then at the envelope. He reaches for his letter opener.

Saks: "Be careful Sol; remember what they did to White."

Sol: "Stand back." Sherman carefully opens the envelope but the only thing in it is a note...

There's a way out. Meet me tonight, 8:00 PM, at the Montmartre Bistro and bring everything. – Grace Edwards.
PS: I was Will's fiancée.

Sherman hands Saks the note.

THE END GAME

Montmartre Bistro

Saks and Sherman walk into the Montmartre at precisely 8:00 PM. Leon Bailey recognizes them immediately.

Leon Bailey: "They're waiting. Follow me."

Bailey takes them to a table in the far corner of the restaurant. Sitting at the table is a very attractive woman and a middle-aged man with balding grey hair and beard dressed in a black turtleneck sweater and expensive charcoal grey suit. Bobby Bloom stands to greet them.

Grace: "Thank you for coming…"

Sherman: "You're Grace Edwards?"

Grace: "Yes, please sit." Sherman and Saks sit.

Bloom: "Have you eaten? I can have Leon bring you something."

Sherman: "And you are?"

Grace: "This is Mr. Bloom. He owns the Montmartre."

Sherman: "Yah, I've heard of you. You work for Bernardo."

Bloom: "Let's just say he's a client."

Sherman: "So what's this all about?"

Bloom: "Miss Edwards and Mr. Bernardo asked me to look into her fiancé's murder."

Saks: "So you know it's a murder?"

Bloom: "As you already know, Smith killed Major White because of the Incident Report he filed and subsequently sent you."

Sherman: "Nobody will publish the story."

Bloom: "That's the least of your problems. They want the evidence and they want you two marginalized."

Saks: "Marginalized? What does that mean?"

Bloom: "Nothing good I'm afraid. They even threatened me."

Grace: "We have a way out, but first we have to turn over the evidence."

Saks and Sherman look at one another.

Sherman: "You think we're idiots. You're working for Smith."

Grace: "Listen, Bobby's on our side. We can get the story out... not the way you intended, but maybe even a better way."

Bloom: "First we have to deal with Smith. Did you bring the evidence?"

Saks reaches into her purse and pulls out a manila envelope containing the original Incident Report and the surveillance disc. She places it on the table.

Bloom: "Copies?"

Sherman reaches into his jacket.

Bloom: "No! Not now... we have plans for that."
Bloom signals Bailey with a wave of his hand. Leon picks up the phone on his podium style reception desk and dials a number. Thirty seconds later a black Ford pulls up in front of the restaurant and Smith gets out. He enters the restaurant and

Bailey shows him to Bloom's table. Bailey doesn't move but stands directly behind Smith.

Bailey: "Don't do anything foolish, Mr. Smith. I would hate to get blood all over the floor. Doesn't look good for the paying customers."

Smith: "I really don't like the service in this place."

Bloom: "Yes, you mentioned that once before."

Smith: "Is that it?"

Bloom: "Yes, that's it."

Smith looks directly at Saks and Sherman.

Smith: "I hope you weren't dumb enough to make copies, but even if you did, it won't do you any good. It will be the equivalent of that ridiculous autopsy video. You might as well quit well your ahead."

Smith reaches for the package but Grace grabs it. She stands up and faces Smith with the envelope in her left hand. With her right fist she hits Smith so hard he actually stumbles over backwards falling to the floor.

Grace: "I hope you rot in hell."

Grace drops the package on top of Smith, who staggers to his feet rubbing his jaw. He makes a move towards Grace but Bailey steps in front blocking his way. The whole restaurant is watching.

Smith then turns to Saks and Sherman. "Your career as journals is finished. Nobody will touch you two with a ten-foot pole, so whatever wild and crazy story you spin, people will just think you're nuts." Smith still rubbing his jaw turns and leaves.

EPILOGUE
Redemption

Grauman's Chinese Theatre, Premiere of "The Incident Report"

Ricky Saks, Sol Sherman, Grace Edwards, and Arnie and Lonnie Bernardo are sitting in the theatre at the Premiere of Bernardo Production's new movie "The Incident Report" starring Grace Edwards as Ricky Saks. The opening title fades and a scrolling text introduction with voice-over appears on screen.

Voiceover: *"On a clear summer's day Air Force test pilot and war hero, Major Willard White flew his final mission. The movie you are about to see is true."*

The movie begins with a re-enactment of Smith spiking White's water in the debriefing room. Cut to the final scene re-enacting the Montmartre meeting.

The group are in the lobby being congratulated by friends and fielding questions from the press. Sherman turns to Saks.

Sherman: "Well, it's not the Pulitzer…"

Saks: "But we got the story out, and we'll probably reach an even bigger audience than if we would have published with a digital dump."

Sherman: "We may not be journalists anymore partner, but the movie business ain't so bad."

Saks: "The pay is certainly better. Now lets go home and really celebrate." She takes Sherman's hand and they leave the theatre while Grace and the Bernardo's pose for pictures.

THE END

ABOUT THE AUTHOR

Jerry Bader is Senior Partner at MRPwebmedia.com, a media production company that specializes in Web video, audio, music, and sound design. Mr. Bader has written and produced dozens of video commercials for clients. Writing scripts and novels is a natural extension that grew out of the experience of creating attention-grabbing mini movies that focus on the core emotional motivator.

Over the years Mr. Bader has written over a hundred articles on marketing, and he's self-published marketing e-books, hybrid graphic novels, biographies, and a series of children's books. The Neo Noir Hybrid Graphic Novels are story concepts developed with the goal of having them turned into television series or feature films. There are currently ten screenplays, five of which have been self-published as hybrid graphic novels: *The Method, The Comeuppance, The Coffin Corner, Grist For The Mill* and *The Black Crane.*

He's also written *The Fixer* published by Rebel Seed Entertainment. It has consistently been in the top ten percent in several Amazon categories. *The Fixer* is based on the true-life story of a colorful horse racing character. The follow-up to *The Fixer* is the new book *Beating The System* that continues the story of the horse racing legend. Mr. Bader has also written *Organized Crime Queens, The Secret World of Female Gangsters, What's Your Poison? How Cocktails Got Their Names, The Outlaw Rider,* and the soon to be released: *Dead End, Palermo, Stone Cold, The Aussie Switch, and Ballet Of Bullets.* Mr. Bader has also written a series of children's books, ZaZa Books For Kids, that currently includes, *Two Dragons Named Shoe, The Town That Didn't Speak, The Criminal McBride, The Bad Puppeteer, Mr. Bumbershoot, The Umbrella Man, The Ninth Inning,* and *14 Ridiculous Tales of Sage Silliness.*

www.ingramcontent.com/pod-product-compliance
Lightning Source LLC
Chambersburg PA
CBHW061306210726
48293CB00003B/1131